Books by Marina Warner

NONFICTION:

Joan of Arc: The Image of Female Heroism   1981
Queen Victoria's Sketchbook   1980
The Crack in the Teacup   1979
Alone of All Her Sex: The Myth and Cult of the Virgin Mary   1976
The Dragon Express   1971

FICTION:

The Skating Party   1983
In a Dark Wood   1977

The Skating Party

The Skating Party

Marina Warner

Atheneum   New York   1983

Library of Congress Cataloging in Publication Data

Warner, Marina,———
    The skating party.

    I. Title.
PR6073.A7274S5   1983   823'.914   82-73007
ISBN 0-689-11368-4

6.82

WAR
130081

FOR RENI

I would not then be left by thee, deare sonne, begot in love –
No, not if God would promise me to raze the prints of time
Carv'd in my bosome and my browes and grace me with the prime
Of manly youth as when at first I left sweet Helle's shore,
Deckt with faire Dames, and fled the grudge my angrie father bore;
Who was the faire Amyntor cald, surnam'd Ormenides,
And for a faire-haird harlot's sake, that his affects could please,
Contemnd my mother his true wife, who ceaslesse urged me
To use his harlot Clytia, and still would claspe my knee
To do her will – that so my Sire might turne his love to hate
Of that lewde Dame, converting it to comfort her estate.

Chapman's translation of *The Iliad*, Book IX

1

On the Floe

I

The Floe last froze over fifteen years ago. The old man with pink cheeks and prophet hair stood on the ice and remembered how that winter he had skated alongside Swash's Dyke all the way to the cathedral. It was Epiphany; the crocketed spire guided him across the frosted fen, and when he reached the town, the boys' choir was singing.

Michael Lovage beside him on the narrow river listened, his head on one side. They were standing together by the glittering stone pier of a bridge and had met by chance, as Wilton was crossing the river to the south bank and the college garden. Michael looked over his glasses invitingly, and asked Professor Wilton if he would like to join his party, skating in the other direction, towards Hartbridge. Then, while the older man considered his answer, Michael began wiping the lenses on his scarf. Wilton's pace was stately by comparison; Michael was in a fever of rush and business.

'Perhaps,' replied Wilton. But first he would see that enough straw had been packed around the roots of the tender climbers to withstand the long winter snap. 'If all is well, I should greatly enjoy a skating party!' He smiled too in answer, his cheeks bright from the cold. 'But clematis and plumbago first.'

Did Professor Wilton have skates? Michael asked. Yes, well greased, and still in the newspaper in which they were wrapped by the college servant during that same cold spell fifteen years ago.

Moving slowly on the marbled river, Wilton slipped from his colleague. As he turned away, his long white hair eclipsed the morning sun that was hanging low and white in the clotted sky, and became an aureole, while through the gaps of his papery fingers the silver radiance of the sun's frosted bulb glowed, incandescent.

Little warmth came from this sun; yet its light was beautiful. The lawn stretching down to the rounded river bank beside the bridge where Michael stood was yielding up its buried greenness in eddies; the viridian brightness of the blades, where the hoar frost lay threadbare, was the only colour to strike the eye and all the more brilliant for its singularity. The melting was negligible, reflected Michael; the sun feeble; frost still lay on the ice like a dusting of fine sugar. The mass under his feet was at least nine inches thick, and the mist, translucent near the sun but yeasty in other parts of the sky, would protect the skaters from the disappointment of a sudden thaw. His shoes hung round his neck, tied together by their laces, over the soft plaid scarf Viola had given him, and his heavy old tweed overcoat. The skating boots pinched his ankles, the heat of the constriction fighting with the cold in his toes. He remembered the sensation wonderingly, the frozen loch in Perthshire at his granny's, the hiss of the blades on the ice.

Strange, he thought, how the body has a memory of things the mind loses. He found he could move with ease, sweeping out left, right, left, feeling the rhythm establishing itself without volition on his part. No, he told himself, the body does not forget.

From the path leading to the bridge, a figure hailed him.

'Jimmy!' Michael shouted up in greeting. He gesticulated, 'Come down.' His breath hung in the air for a moment like a wraith.

Two men were skittering down the slope, blackening its layer of frosted snow with their clumsy tracks. The younger of the two now jumped down on to the river, laughed when it took his weight without a creak and held out his hand to his companion, who leaning on it was lowering himself more cautiously on to the ice.

'I must say, very fancy,' said Jimmy, eyeing Michael swivelling to a standstill in front of them. 'We managed to hire some skates.' He buried his chin in his muffler. 'For me, and for Andrew here. Andrew luckily has small feet, and I've got large. There's been a huge demand for the average sizes.' He emphasised his words as if intending double entendres; innuendo was a habit of speech. He looked up at Michael mischievously. 'Neither of us have done it before. I don't know if we'll manage your ...' He dipped his shoulders and swayed his portly hips. 'Most fetching. Something to be said for those Spartan children's hols, after all.'

Andrew blew on his hands and then tucked them into the pockets of the short blue sanforized wind-cheater he was wearing.

'You should have some gloves,' said the older man, solicitously. 'Shall I fetch a pair from my rooms?' He began to scramble up the bank again.

'No, no.' Andrew touched Jimmy's leg. 'I'm fine. I'm used to it. You know. Remember? I work like this.' He spread his hands and smiled, pleasantly. In turn he dipped his shoulders and swayed. 'When we get going, I'll warm up.'

The three men laughed agreeably together, and looked across at the sharp white disc of the sun. It was tangled in willow fronds that, rimed in sparkling white, were stilled, as in a time pause, their fingertips trapped by the river's crust of ice.

'Who's coming?' asked Jimmy.

'Mostly students.' For an instant, Katy's face pierced Michael's mind's eye, like a flare at sea. 'Mostly *my* students,' he lied.

'No!' said Jimmy. 'How noble!'

Andrew helped to pull Jimmy up the bank on the other side, to a bench where they could change into their skating boots. From the river, Michael called up to them, 'Remember, lace them so tight it hurts. That's the only way you'll manage to stand up in them.'

'Oh God,' groaned Jimmy. 'I can't think why I agreed to this.'

'You wanted me to meet your friends, right?' said Andrew. He coquetted in front of the older man on the bench. 'Wanted to show me off.'

'Really,' said Jimmy. But he was smiling.

A slim woman standing on the bridge waved at them. 'Here we are, darling!' Viola called. Her voice, clear and precise, carried well. The dark, sharp-faced boy beside her did not wave like his mother, but swung himself on to the parapet of the bridge and threw off his shoes.

From the bank, Jimmy wagged a hand. Viola smiled back, tossing her head. Her thick hair was loose, except for a clip to one side, and fell in strands over the turned-up fur collar of her belted gaberdine coat.

'You'll get wet, Timmo,' she said to her son. 'Sitting in the wet.'

'I'll dry soon enough,' he answered.

'Can you manage it too?' Jimmy, leaning anxiously against Andrew, asked Timmo who now joined them on skates. 'I'm the wrong generation, I can see.' He looked at Viola's son with keen pleasure.

'Yeah,' said Timmo, 'the roller generation. And ice skating is easier, I reckon.'

'I'll need your help.' Jimmy lurched against Andrew.

Viola was dashing from the bank to join them; she braked with a sharp turn that sent up a small spray of ice from each blade. 'Of course. We'll escort you, Timmo and I, one on each side.' She circled the group and drew her arm through Jimmy's. 'There, we're all set. Michael!' She turned her head over her shoulder as she called out. Her breath, exhaled in the sharp air, rose milkily before her face, softening its already soft contours like a photographer's gauze. Her nose and cheeks were rosy, but the high colour suited her, and she looked over at her husband where he stood in a knot of new arrivals for the expedition. Then she caught her son's eye and smiled at him encouragingly. His dark long eyes, with the slight crookedness of set that he had inherited from her, were puzzled, and the line of his wide mouth was grudging.

'Timmo,' she began, restrainingly, but cared more not to intrude on his mood than to change it for the sake of the gathering.

'You're okay?' Timmo asked, unthreading his arm from Jimmy's where his mother had placed it. 'I'll just go and say hello.' He left them, with a nonchalant wave from the hip.

'You too,' said Jimmy to Viola. 'Go and greet your guests.'

'I'll be back.' Viola set off, gliding, after her son.

From the back, mother and son resembled each other strikingly. At just seventeen he had outstripped her, but he was slightly built too, and his thin legs and sharp jutting knees stuck out through his trousers so that, even when he was standing up, his legs never looked quite straight, and this gait replicated his mother's, in a manner Michael found touching. Especially in high heels, Viola's bent legs reminded Michael of the flamingo's stooping walk, and he used the bird's name to his wife sometimes in affection. Yet Viola gave an impression of alertness and control all the same, while Timmo looked angered by the disobedience of his gawky limbs.

'Hello, darling,' said Michael, as Viola came up with the hiss of a tearing sheet as again she stopped on the ice in a spindrift of frost from the points of her skates. 'We've got some fairly unversed skaters here,' he said. But Michael was not apologetic; he clearly saw the outing as a challenge.

'We've been practising,' said a girl with long fair hair, 'since the frost began, and Dr Lovage began planning this.'

'Michael,' he protested. 'Please call me Michael.'

He went round the circle giving names. Viola did not shake hands, but nodded, smiling generously, conscious with a certain happy confidence that Michael's students were often abashed by her attractiveness, because the wife of a don, let alone a member of the teaching faculty, was meant to be dowdy and plain. How slow to change prejudices are, she thought as she unclipped the slide and loosened her wavy brown hair. Then, striking out with one foot, she spun around. Timmo, behind her, said 'Hi' sullenly to the group, his long eyes sliding sideways. 'I for one am off,' she cried.

As Viola sped back to Jimmy, one small, peaky, tense face in the ring around her husband stuck in her mind's eye. The girl's pale-blue eyes were rimmed with kohl, but even its heaviness could not veil the naïve avidity with which she had looked at Viola. This open and unmasked curiosity, mixed with a prideful desire to show no interest, had produced on the young girl's white face a transparent expression of conflict that went far beyond the surprise Viola so often relished when she met some-one who had expected her to be different.

The girl's lips were whitened in the latest fashion, and thin and firm above a pointed chin. She had a silver star on her cheek, just below the corner of her mouth, and the ends of spiky, shoulder-length hair dyed jet black poked out of a knitted cap with a design of dolls along its edge. In spite of, as well as because of the fashionable paint, it was an interesting face. Its naked register of hurt compelled Viola, and she turned to look again at the group. The girl was in a short cape, of black silky material, and under it she wore a looseknit saffron sweater to her thighs, belted at the waist over a short scarlet skirt and black trousers so skin-tight they resembled hose. She was smoking a cigarette, uncomfortably, holding it between mittened fingers with an awkwardness that betrayed a lack of custom, and puff-ing it in such a way that she declared with each puff how keenly she wanted to look worldly and depraved. She stood stiffly to one side, and Michael, opposite her, seemed almost to prance on the ice, like a fresh pony before a new rider. Viola put her head on one side, and nodded to herself. She had seen that friskiness before.

With her arm through Jimmy's again, she forced a smile. 'Timmo gets more gorgeous every day,' he teased. 'Can't wait for him to grow up.'

'Really!' She squeezed his arm. 'Still lots of crosspatch teenage stuff. But it'd be more worrying if he just loved everything Mum and Dad did, wouldn't it? That's the problem. Who wants a placid, well-behaved, eager, obedient child? No one.'

'A bit of delinquency is what you like, is it?'

'Come now.'

'I know, I know, he's the best son in the whole world.'

'Do you know, I think he is.' Viola shook her head again and looked hard at Jimmy. With sudden vehemence, she made a profession to her friend, that she could not imagine what her life would have been like if Timmo had not existed. She said, 'He's the only thing I can take straight on, without feeling set apart.'

She was a watcher, who understood the act of looking on. That was why she liked painting, why she understood painters. But, with a pang, she recognised how she was kept on the sidelines by her faculty. 'Timmo is the only element in my life that really involves me,' she added. She found such self-definition through motherhood rather sad, but unavoidable somehow.

Andrew joined in, 'Stroll on! My ma'd think you came from another planet.' He cut his throat with a gesture. 'She was completely fed up to here with us kids.'

Viola controlled the sympathy that sprung instantly in her. 'It's not true,' she said.

'Yeah. It's true,' muttered Andrew.

Michael skated over to them. A map fluttered in his hand. He stabbed at it, once spread, to show them the route to Hartbridge.

'What planning!' said Jimmy. 'I didn't know you had this General Staff stuff in you, Michael.'

A raggle taggle of young people was passing, braced one against the other, with joined hands and linked arms.

'We're kind of off,' giggled a skater, one of Michael's graduate students. He wiped a cold drop from his nose, and grinned as his companion faltered when she lost his steadying grip. With yells and laughter, the line weaved and stumbled as the braver members began pushing themselves forward on the ice.

'I'm just not moving,' wailed the fair-haired girl.

'You'll be fine,' soothed her support.

'I suppose you spent every winter vac skiing,' said the girl bitterly.

'Sun and surf down by the ocean, ski and snow up in the San Bernardino Mountains. Dandy.' He held her arm as the line, spreading across the river, broke into groups of twos and threes. 'I'll give you a hand.'

Michael, seeing his guests on their way, was circling round to weave through them to his son.

'Try and enjoy yourself,' he ordered.

Timmo's mouth curved down. 'Yeah, yeah.' He sped off with arms held low and knees bent to overtake his mother.

'Lovage!' came a cry from the bank.

'I'm delighted,' Michael said in greeting. He helped hand Wilton down the bank on to the ice. 'Clematis all fixed up nicely?'

'Yes, yes. Nelly Moser a little exposed at the roots, but I soon remedied that,' murmured the old man, and with his hands clasped behind his back, his snowy head tilted slightly at an angle to his inclined torso, he began, with smooth sliding steps, to gain on the group of Michael's guests as they disappeared under the elegant, high-humped arabesque of the second, modern bridge along the Floe. Michael paused to contemplate Wilton in admiration, and then at an abrupt, energetic pace, caught up with the swanlike old man.

'What a master!' he said.

'You never forget such things.'

'No, but you do have to do them well in the first place.'

And they skated on side by side.

The skaters were moving like space voyagers in the void of whiteness; their cries and their shouts and their laughter thrummed, magnified in the silence as if the low, white sky were padded with soundproofing cloud. The stone college buildings across the lawn that shelved down to the river seemed discoloured ivory against the blazing whiteness of the snowladen scene. Every twig and branch of the sparse sedge and alders that now sprouted along the river's edge was coated in sparkling crystals, clustered tight as filings on a magnet. Aslant the whiteness poured the creamy curd light of the winter sun, setting here and there a facet of the hoar frost glinting like diamonds. Now and then, as the skaters passed, a moorhen hopped on the frozen surface.

In the ice beneath the skaters' feet, bubbles were frozen in swirls, and a craquelure, as on an old canvas, forked through the slabby ice-crust. On this flawed opaline surface, the skaters' slicing blades cut trails of ice powder with a flash of metal and a sharp sigh of blade against crystal; they crossed and recrossed in an interwoven pattern, sometimes a restless and impatient scribble, sometimes lazy as the undulations of kite tails on a breeze.

The crunch of the surface was the most living sound the skaters heard; the occasional plop, when the struggling sun managed to loose one snowflake from its matrix, was desolate.

Yet the skaters were not melancholy in this lulled world; rather they felt transported by its uncanniness, by the petrification of familiar sights, by the still buildings majestically moored on a blank wilderness. They shouted to one another how pleased they were Michael had forced them out, they chaffed the stumblers and the cautious, they praised the flashing proficiency of the fleet-footed, they puffed against the cold, and their cries rose in white steam and disappeared into the close white canopy of the sky.

The first bridge's spans had been within reach of the tallest skaters as they passed underneath. Never very high, especially in summer when the river level fell, the current was swollen with ice, so that even short Jimmy Gattingly was able to touch the keystone. After the second bridge, the buildings of another college crowded down to the river's edge, and Michael's guests were floating past red-brick walls where lichens clung in stars of frost. For a time they heard one another's voices sound off the stones as if at a great distance underground in a cavern.

2

Make-believe with Timmo had often lacked point. Viola, some-times cross she couldn't enter wholly into play, without a need for other justification, would still be unable to concentrate al-together on the part of Sheriff or Pilot or Detective or Spaceman. Timmo would reproach her with absent-mindedness; his look of disappointment when she did not immediately expire in a heap at the end of his gun would force her to greater, even more delighting death throes.

Once, ten years ago in Palau, the game had meant something more to Viola. It had excited her, to conspire with Timmo against the priests' power in the island, even though she had been ashamed to use him as her dupe.

She was saying to him: 'Let's play make-believe.'

'Yes, let's.' The little boy's smile flashed in his face, already, at seven, often solemn and preoccupied.

She adjusted the scarf around her forehead in an Indian band. 'You be the pathfinder and I'll be the Chief.' Seeing the rebellion in Timmo's face, Viola instantly backtracked. 'No, you be Chief, and I'll be . . .'

'You're my squaw,' said the child firmly. 'And I'm Big Chief Whiteface.'

They were in a coconut grove. Its tall palms gave little shade; the steamy heat wrapped them softly, like a scarf.

'Now, squaw, you take that side. I'll take this.' Timmo ges-tured towards the temple precinct in front of them, and dashed to a tree, taking cover behind its trunk.

Pressing a finger to her lips, Viola beckoned him back. 'It's too dangerous to separate. We stick together now, Big Chief.'

'Okay,' he said. He crouched down and ran forward along the

ground, as if ducking fire. From a new coconut, he turned and signalled to her to follow.

'Can you see the hostage?' she asked.

Timmo clasped the tree's smooth slim trunk and slowly poked his head around.

'I see nothing move.' He twisted back, and began scampering across the sandy soil of the grove towards his mother. 'There's going to be an ambush. We must be very careful.' His brown eyes danced with excitement.

'Do you think so? Not if we move very, very quietly.' Viola was serious. 'Let's make another approach. This way.'

They skirted the temple boundary, marked out by a shallow depression, a symbolic fosse, between the sand and the earth floor on which the cluster of ritual buildings stood. Squat shadows cast by the granite stupas of the sanctuary lay across the empty enclave. Viola and Timmo ran, zigzagging from one tree to another until, clasped together in excitement, they peered around the palm tree that stood nearest to the back wall of the main temple building in the compound.

Timmo looked up at his mother. He wore diagonal crimson stripes made with her lipstick on his cheeks. 'Shall we storm it with our braves?' he asked.

'We haven't made certain of the position of the captive,' she answered. 'We'll have to send in a scout.'

'I'll be the scout,' said Timmo, determinedly, and was off, running low, to the wall of the building. He followed it round, until it met the shallow ditch, then threw himself face down on the ground.

'Over here.' He waved an arm above his head.

Viola sauntered towards him, treading softly in her sandals. Behind her, a heavy thud suddenly broke the silence. She jumped, and shrieked, 'Timmo!'

Timmo shifted on to his elbows, and made a face at his mother: don't break the rules, it said.

Viola realised it was only a coconut falling and hitting earth. But her heart still thumped. She dropped on all fours and crawled over to her son.

'There's the hostage, look.' The child jerked his head towards the verandah of the open temple. The screen doors were parted, to reveal a small, bare interior striped with light through the slatted blinds.

Viola saw the girl. She was sitting on the floor, on a mat, with her legs tucked under her, and a sarong swathed tight around the graceful curves of her slim body.

Viola's breath came sharply. She had not expected to find her at all, and to find her like this, alone and apparently unguarded, was startling. Her detention was a compact then between the priests who held her, and the girl herself. If she wanted, she could clearly leave.

Viola motioned to Timmo to stay still. Her game, using him, scared her now. As she watched, she saw the girl pick up the bowl of water at her side and bend her face towards its mirroring surface. Then she put the bowl down again and, unfastening the turtleshell comb in her hair, let her long black hair fall and began to smooth it. Then she lifted it and with the same comb secured it with a single twist of her wrist.

Viola stood up, slowly, ready to drop instantly to the ground if she turned out to be mistaken, and a guard did appear. No, there was no sign of anyone else.

Timmo looked up at his mother, impatiently. 'Can't we attack now?' He hit each word hard, pleading.

'Yes, of course.'

Viola turned her head, as if to a detachment behind them. 'Ready?' she called out.

'That's my part,' wailed Timmo.

'Darling, I'm sorry.'

'Ready?' he piped, recovering. He slotted an imaginary arrow to an imaginary bow, took aim, pulled back and let the arrow fly. His eyes described its arc through the air. With a whoop he ran forward, into the temple.

Viola stayed back. Her eyes were on the girl. She was checking her dressed hair in the water bowl. Viola saw her as, startled, she raised her head. Timmo, giving Indian war cries, careered across the compound towards her. Water splashed on the verandah floor as she jumped to her feet.

Viola then shouted out, as loudly as she could, 'Timmo, come back here, Timmo!' The girl's glance flew from the child to the woman, as Viola had hoped. Viola waved, took the bundle of food from her belt, where she had fastened it, and held it up for a moment. Then she laid it on the ground and kicked some sand over it.

The girl fluttered in the light between the verandah and her quarters' shadowy interior. Her slim hands made gestures of terror and she backed away behind the screen, deep in the darkness of the hut.

Had she seen Viola's action? Had she grasped its meaning?

Timmo, at the girl's fright, stopped in his tracks; now he wandered back, sulkily kicking up the sand with his feet.

'You scared her. You spoilt it,' he said.

Viola rumpled her son's hair. 'I don't think she wanted to play.'

3

Viola sped up to her son, but refrained from linking arms with him. He no longer liked her to touch him.

She remembered when shame, the mark of Timmo's adulthood, began to keep them apart, and the excitement mixed with melancholy that it stirred in her. It was nine-thirty one night; Viola found the airing cupboard overflowing with clothes taken slightly damp from the washing line and then laid in a jumble over the soft red lagging of the boiler jacket. She sorted out Michael's linen, her own, the tea towels and tablecloth to go back downstairs. She made a pile too of clothes from her son's wardrobe: his wide-striped cotton rugby shirts, inside out and looking as if they had suffered ten years' wear and tear, his jeans, carefully boiled on the kitchen stove in the spaghetti cauldron, his odd socks, felted at the foot, one or two underpants. Holding against her body the armful of clothes with their smell of warmed detergent, she turned the handle of the door to his room, pushed it open with her shoulder, and so entered crabwise, without looking ahead, without the polite alertness of a guest, with the familiarity and heedlessness of the hotel chambermaid who passes into strangers' rooms and breaks into their intimacies without compunction or surprise. But Timmo was yelling at her. Not words, but a throaty, animal horror. As she swiftly closed the door again, she said, 'Sorry, darling.' The phrase clashed, improbably genteel, with the strangled fury of his final articulated cry: 'Get out of here. Get out of my room!'

He was standing naked, looking at himself in the mirror. When she closed the door, Viola could not bring herself to walk away immediately. She stood on the landing, and the grin that broke open on her face mingled with an infuriating pricking in her eyes.

Her son, her baby Timmo whose limbs she had smoothed and fondled, whose body she had bathed and patted, slapped and teased, tickled and bitten, hugged and kissed, had passed beyond the reach of her permitted caress. She raised a hand to her forehead and then over her eyes, rubbing the tears that held in a corner of her lid and laughing, with no sound.

He had been looking at the flesh stem of his penis where it rose from a tangle of light furze; he was holding himself and standing sideways to the glass, taking in the angle of its growth. Before his face became convulsed with horror at her presence, behind him in the reflection it had blazed with a greedy, self-glorying radiance, through slitted eyes and clenched teeth.

From then on, Viola knocked at the door of her son's room. He kissed her sometimes, arriving back from school, but peckingly, and their bodies never touched. And though all this was sad after the long intimacy of his childhood, it felt inside Viola like a triumph. His new sexed existence separated them; but she felt that his sexuality belonged to her, that it was her experience by right.

Viola and Timmo skated along together side by side for a few moments. Viola knew better than to exacerbate Timmo's earlier sullenness by commenting on it. She kept silent, giving him a barely perceptible smile. His cheeks were glowing from the keen air; she looked tenderly at the dark pinpoints of the new stubble, just defining the jawline and the point of his chin. He returned his mother's look for a moment, and she was proud then too of the intelligent directness of his dark, quick eyes.

At length he spoke: 'Perhaps it's not a lemon after all.'

'What isn't?'

Timmo gestured at the white willows, the quiet buildings, the moving skaters on the river, the snowy pillows on the quoins of the first bridge behind them.

'Did you think it would be?' Viola shook her head at him.

'Sure,' Timmo cut back. Then he laughed. 'If Dad had gone over the route one more time, I'd have pissed off.'

'Your father's a very good planner.'

'A fusser, you mean.'

Viola did not defend Michael, in spite of Timmo's tone. The triangular tension that sustained her family, like tent cords which strain one against the other for the kingpost to stand, was familiar to Viola since Timmo's birth, and she acknowledged that it was only Michael's easy-going nature and lack of envy that prevented the tug of Timmo's existence from bringing down the structure. Michael tolerated their child's claim on her; she could not reciprocate, and when Timmo as an infant was taken from her arms and carried in his father's, she had felt a stab of loss and sometimes even a surge of anger. Michael had participated in the drama of her bond with the baby like a genial understudy who watches a central performance he will only take over in exceptional circumstances; but Viola, when he wanted to help her, felt a conflict between the respite Michael's fathering offered her, and jealousy that her special tie, this union she felt with the child, might be frayed by their closeness.

Michael, in his turn, felt the strain, not in longing to share Viola's motherhood, but as impatience with the time-consuming nature of her involvement. He wanted her attention too, for himself, at times when Timmo, rampant at the table, majestic in his occupation of his parents' bed, was set on absorbing all of it. She laughed to herself, briefly, as she recalled when the three-year-old, not content at placing himself between his mother and his father in bed, had sometimes peed sleepily into the mattress, as effective a restraint as Tristan's naked sword. But sometimes Michael's want of her filled her with guilt, and she felt sundered by the rivalry between Timmo and his father; while at other times, when Michael surrendered his place with wry, mild effacement, she felt cheated by the self-sufficiency in him that could make her superfluous.

Timmo was Viola's second pregnancy. The first, happening in her third term at university soon after she began sleeping with Michael, had brought them very close in mutual dismay. Michael, twenty years old, was enveloped in that gossip, both malicious and admiring, that clung midge-like around leading figures in the university's activities. The national dailies, greedy to report subversion amongst the most privileged youth of the nation, frequently extracted his speeches at demonstrations, and gave him, as he walked in the narrow streets of the town, a certain notoriety. He was known to many whom he did not know, and, amongst them, Viola.

She met him on the street, under a lamp-post by the covered market's decorative ironwork porch. He was swinging past on his bicycle, and had a sheaf of papers under one arm. The other was hanging loose, with conscious nonchalance. Seeing Viola's companion, a fellow campaigner against the building of a local nuclear missile site, he swerved to a halt. When he began speaking, his words were abrupt and earnest, but there was a devilry in his deep voice and in the creases around his wide extrovert mouth that made him thrilling to her then. And the authority of his réclame, his energy, his young, opinionated, greedy intelligence, was compounded for Viola by his size. Without shoes, she came eye-level with his chest. She was made insignificant, and she liked it. His unaccustomed hands first stroked her hair, long then as now, with a callow and urgent hunger, and she felt as if she were expanding out of herself, flying out of the narrow cell of her small body and spinning up a vortex of bright stars. But later when, after the two weeks of waiting, she faced him to tell him she was having a baby, he parted with his careless dominance as with a borrowed costume and appeared to be so scared and helpless that Viola felt almost serene by contrast.

Michael and she hardly spoke about their decision, but he travelled with her to London on the train, and then to a stop on the Northern line in the sprawl of the great city neither of them knew. She phrased the event to herself as an accident, something like a killing in a car. She was unable to acknowledge that she herself had chosen to have the baby aborted, responsibly and consciously. No, the death was something that had happened to her. She had been propelled, somnambulist, into the mean waiting-room where months' old magazines were piled, dirty and dog-eared, and the other women lowered their eyes and did not speak. Viola kept her eyes on the goldfish in the fishtank, in which three guppies flapped their fins to stay against the smeared glass.

No possibility this is a lasting relationship?, the woman doctor asked. She was smoking wearily; the roots of her hair were grey. Viola shook her head. She was choking. Still as if in sleep, she walked down the tunnel of the tube on her way to another northern suburb, where the Nursing Home was placed. She felt her limbs were dropping off her trunk with soft rottenness, and the only green, hard fruit in her was being torn away, unripe and stunted. A windfall of the spring.

Afterwards, in the heavy clarity of her returned consciousness, she became desolate. She sat in the waiting-room with the other girls, waiting for Michael to come and take her back to college, and a jangling chumminess stole through the group as the men turned up one by one. They giggled in acceptance of the community between them. A shared touch of death had released them all.

Michael was pale when he arrived, and stood awkwardly in the doorway. He held her outside in a silent, unhappy embrace that was so unlike his usual effervescent and teasing articulateness she felt again bound to him, adrift in that starlit vortex.

So when she conceived again eighteen months later, though they had tried to be careful, but were clumsy and inhibited by rubbers and jelly, she could not undergo another abortion. Michael was cheerful and confident, and took her to see the tiny flats his enlightened college had recently built for married postgraduates. He touched her stomach, saying, 'Poor bugger, with parents like us.' She was shocked at her child's immediately separate existence in his imagination; from the start for her the baby was incorporated as one with her.

The baby gave her a great boon, fairy gold: her loving could never suffice him. She never had to restrain herself, put a check on her demonstrativeness. But she gradually became disloyal to her lover his father. Loving him or any adult demanded so much more consideration of the other's feelings and opinions. She let her son as he grew up keep his father at a distance with criticisms that began as tests on his good nature and a search for boundaries, but became irritable impatience as Timmo developed into a clever, restless boy.

'Dad is so pompous!' This was Timmo, after Michael acquitted himself well under fire from a colleague about a recent paper he had submitted to a journal. 'Why does he take himself so seriously?' It was the first time Viola heard their son detach himself so clearly from his father's alliance and she was at first alarmed. But his absence of identification with his father soon acquired a subtle, pleasant flavour, and she and Timmo became conspirators. It surprised her, how easy it was to play a double role. She sympathised with her husband, and, with the oblique ironies he liked, she indulged the very foibles, mannerisms and reactions that most provoked her son's intolerance; and at the same time, she played deliciously the ever-growing drama of collusion with Timmo, as her eyes met his over the kitchen table and rolled, just slightly, at some absolutely characteristic Michael-ish remark. 'I called the man in Geneva, and I told him, straight, that it was a perversion, yes, a perversion, of the democratic process to allow X, Y and Z to get away with using their vote in the X, Y, Z, to upset a measure that has taken five years to get to this point.'

He was admirable, she was filled with pride at Michael's unceasing public-spiritedness, his tireless letter-writing, pamphleteering, lobbying on behalf of issues he saw as moral, higher than political. But she could also see with Timmo's jaded eye (had she perhaps formed it?) the blustering, self-important, and ultimately ineffectual academic Timmo kicked against.

'Suppose you've sent Ahmed Pavli a telegram deploring the massacre,' Timmo said once, aggressive, standing in the hall, hands on his jeans belt.

'Several of us have, to be exact.'

'Fat lot that'll do.'

Michael did not answer. He took in that the massacre of an entire township had shaken Timmo also to tears, and he had given up trying to reconcile their emotional difference by riposte through argument. Viola did not give her husband protection against her son because she did not think he needed it: Timmo's reactions were cussed, not lethal. Or so she judged it.

She struck out now faster on the ice, sweeping forward without remonstrating at his ungrateful disposition towards his father. Skating backwards from her son, she looked past him over his shoulder at the less experienced skaters who were straggling behind.

'I'll give someone a tug,' she said. 'Why don't you too?'

Timmo turned around, a little unsteadily, but holding his balance. 'I might pull them over, you know.'

But his manner was yielding, and so Viola pointed at Andrew and Jimmy. 'Let's talk to Jimmy and Andrew. They'd like it.'

She leaned forward, and with two or three bold gliding steps, drew side by side with Jimmy.

4

Michael held out his hand to help Katy in her skates down on to the river. She ignored his offer. But she did not move away from him when she reached the ice, and he accepted her lingering, however equivocal, with delight.

'Are you cold?' he asked, as they began moving away side by side.

Her black-suited legs moved sawingly. 'No,' she said. Then, after a pause, she added, 'Besides, I like the cold. I like being cold.'

'And I like heat,' replied Michael with a laugh. He liked nothing better than a real tropical climate, he told her, with the air feeling like butter and the earth baked so hot that when the rain came sweeping down, it turned to steam on contact.

Katy looked at him for the first time since they had joined each other at the party. 'I've been in the desert. When I was small, and we were in Aden.' But she didn't remember the weather. 'At least not the feel of it.'

'I suppose children don't. Except', said Michael, putting out a hand to steady Katy, but withdrawing it when he saw her shrink away imperceptibly, 'in heat waves. When I was a child, I used to make a tent with the sheet and see how long it took to deflate, to settle again around me.'

'What I like', said Katy firmly, 'is getting into bed in between sheets that are really fresh.' She emphasised the word, to conjure the chill and purity she meant.

Michael grimaced.

'And then slowly, slowly, feel the warmth grow and wrap me up. My room in college is perfect. It's always subzero if I've been out and the gas's been off.'

Michael looked at her face, trying to decipher the cause of her sudden self-wounding vehemence about the cold. Under her knitted hat, her white skin had acquired a slight pink sheen, and her small, straight nose was red at the tip. For all her attempts to mask herself under the white lipstick and the black eye-liner, her candid expression still showed itself nakedly, and Michael responded to this failed disguise in her with a violent longing to strip down further the layers of her concealment.

'You wouldn't prefer to be sleeping out, so warm that you'd need no covering? You could look up at the stars.'

'No.' Katy hung her head and shuffled on her skates as they hung back to keep pace with Michael's guests. 'I'd feel . . . unsafe.'

'You look very pretty today,' he said, coaxingly.

Katy kept her face averted, but the line of her blanched lips stiffened. 'I don't feel it,' she said.

'Of course, that's all as usual,' Michael continued, with a quick laugh. He wondered if she ever looked plain. 'I'd love to see you look really plain. Ugly. Dirty. Sluttish!'

Katy bit her lip. His heavy gallantry vexed her.

'In Palau with me, all hot and bothered, sweating, and no running water to wash it off.' He laughed and put out a hand towards her, imitating the motion of sponging her down.

'Don't,' she begged.

Michael dropped the teasing tone, 'You know, that's the Needham Professor,' he said seriously, 'of the History of Science.' He nodded towards Wilton's figure, moving smoothly, behind them.

'Is he? What does that mean?' She spoke disconnectedly. 'Besides, you know it's impossible.'

'What?' said Michael, too quickly.

She looked again at him, her eyes brimming. 'We couldn't be in Palau.'

'My sweet,' Michael said gently, 'that doesn't mean I don't want it.'

Katy replied, her tone less testy, 'No, I suppose not.'

When Michael first met Katy he had immediately felt impelled to scrutinise her, to find the child face concealed underneath her mask of paint.

'Watch it,' she had said, calmly, when his need to pore over her features made him, on that first occasion, veer dangerously close to a bicyclist.

Katy, with her thumb raised for a lift, no umbrella, hat or scarf, was standing in a steady drizzle one March morning the year before as Michael was driving into college. He often stopped for students on his way in and, mechanically, he drew to a halt just beyond Katy and leaned over to open the front passenger seat door for her. She pushed her wet fringe out of her eyes with bare hands and thanked him brusquely without looking him in the eye; then she stamped on the ground to shake off the moisture on her coat and her boots.

'Quick,' he said. 'Jump in.'

An animal smell of wet cloth steamed off her.

Michael had remained optimistic about the calibre of the students, in spite of continual complaints from his colleagues, and he liked making contact with them. Katy was in her first year, she told him, and reading Classics. When Michael commented, 'That's a bit old-fashioned, isn't it?' Katy retorted fast that if he had read Propertius or Catullus or Homer he wouldn't think so. It was then he looked at her, and nearly hit the bicyclist.

'Watch it,' she exclaimed, calm. Then with more force, said, 'They knew it all.'

Michael smiled to himself at how touching it was that a girl in her green years should think that she had enough experience to judge the extent of others'. 'But the world has changed since then, a lot. Surely?'

'People haven't, have they?' She sounded rough, and her bitter tone reminded Michael of his son. 'The same things hurt, then as now. The same things are shitty, aren't they?' When Timmo swore, Michael was furious; but he was flattered that this girl did not defer to his age by cleaning up her language.

She asked him if she might smoke. He told her, lightly, that she should try and give up before the habit hardened.

He produced the phrases by rote, knowing that they would have no effect except to confirm her need for a cigarette. He recognised in her that destructive pride and defiance that Timmo shared, and he spoke with so little conviction that she smiled for the first time and pushed in the lighter on his dashboard. When she smiled, she turned her face towards him, and her teeth, surprisingly large in her small oval face, betrayed a kind of generous humour that she had so far not revealed to him. He smiled back, registering with the deepest pleasure the effect her smile had on him.

Michael Lovage revelled in any new focus for his huge energies; one of the reasons he so often adopted a new friend with whooping abandon was that the investigation of someone's character, past and potential, became for him an irresistible yarn, a kind of pulp adventure in which he could soak himself gleefully and yet experience distantly, on the periphery of his being. He wanted to ask her straightaway what hurt she discovered in the poets she had mentioned; but he knew better than to press her to immediate intimacies, and he reserved the question for a future time. Instead, he exuded warmth and forbearance to her with all his powers, so that he could without heaviness ask her for her name.

She said, 'Katherine. But I'm called Kate, or Katy.'

She didn't ask him his name, but he told her, in full. Katy did not volunteer her surname in response, and there was an amused crease at the corner of her mouth as she understood the niggling effect her reticence was having on him. He, valuing that the coquetry in her sprang from sensing his attraction for her, remained circumspect. So he forbore to push her to identify herself further. But he did ask her, as they approached the main street

where she had asked to be dropped off, if she were taught by one of the Classics dons at her college whom he knew.

'Oh, yes,' she said, almost gaily. She liked this tutor very very much, she told him, and she became more voluble than at any previous moment during the lift. Everything Miss Sidmouth taught came alive. 'She sits on a low stool, by the fireplace, with her brown skirt drawn down over her knees, and she talks and talks. Not always about the subject, and certainly not about my essays.' Katy raised her chin with a wry nod of her head, 'Thank God!'

Michael drew up in the street.

Katy stayed in her seat, and twisted, excitedly, towards him: 'You know that she's the daughter of a man who, well, looked after the money, yes, a wages clerk, at a mine, before the war? And she got a scholarship here, ages ago, when women hardly ever did or could. Just after it happened, she was walking with her mother through the market-place of their town, somewhere up north, and they bumped into a woman.'

Michael looked at Katy patiently.

'Seriously, let me tell you,' she said.

'Go ahead.' He was indulgent.

'This woman had employed Miss Sidmouth's mother as a lady's maid. She had bathed and dressed and, well, done everything for her. When the woman went out, Mrs Sidmouth went with her, in case she needed a stitch here or a pin pushing back in her hair. When they met in the market, she stopped and said straight out: "Sidmouth, your girl will be moving beyond her station. Mr James and Mr Charles went there." ' Katy deepened her voice and chopped her vowels in imitation. 'Isn't that incredible?' She opened the car door and threw her cigarette into the gutter. 'No congratulations at all.'

She didn't wait for Michael's reply, but with a quick, 'Thanks for the ride', she hitched her book bag over her shoulder and pushed the door to. Michael did not search in his mirror to follow her as she made her way down the pavement. But when he looked into it to move out again, she was there, in the centre of his vision, dodging incompetently through the thick of the traffic.

Rowena Sidmouth sat with Michael on a committee that reported to the University Grants Commission; he telephoned her on the pretext of some business and mentioned he had met one of her students. 'Oh yes, Katherine Ordel.' She gave him her name without awareness of the gift. 'An exhibitioner. A girl of some quality. Original, but a bit feckless. So little concentration.' The northern voice was melancholy, beyond the usual toneless-ness of the vowels. 'So many lack application these days.'

'She enjoys your tutorials.'

'Did she say so? Good. But they don't any longer make the most of their time here. Of course, we had a struggle, and it's a good thing it's behind us. But I can't help wishing that the young women now had more of a sense of the past. I wish they appreciated the battle we fought.'

Michael did not comment that he thought that Katy probably did appreciate it. He was afraid to show too much contact. Afterwards he looked at the telephone for a moment and felt ashamed. How much more generous it would have been to forget about protecting himself. With a phrase, he would have given Miss Sidmouth pleasure, and done Katy Ordel justice. And so already his curiosity about Katy developed another facet: he was touched by remorse at his paltriness. And this feeling in turn gave urgency to his desire to see her again, for his own peace of mind, so that he could make amends for his little act of cowardice.

When Michael saw Katy again, it was by chance. Yet in the small university town it was not altogether unlikely. She was walking down the main street by the bookshop. He rushed up to her on the instant without deliberation, as if to pick up an interrupted dialogue. She frowned slightly, not able to place

29

him, and then, because this forgetfulness was rude, was more amenable to his urgent attention than she would have been if that moment of absence had not been visible. He offered her a coffee; she agreed and sat at the table while he queued. He found he could not stop turning his head to make sure that she was still sitting there, alone, isolated from the morning crowd he feared might any moment disclose a friend who would rob him of seclusion with her. Every time he turned his head, he smiled and nodded, reassuring himself and Katy that in spite of the snail's pace of the queue and the lack of teaspoons (they had all disappeared into the scummy waters of the canteen's sink) he would soon be beside her.

When at length, ridiculous smiliness like a tic on his face, he arrived with the tray, the Danish pastries, and two paper napkins, she got up to fetch an ashtray. She had small hands, he noticed, with short nails, and the skin around them was gnawed and pink. When she saw his eyes rest on them, she curled her fingers into her palms and, with a twisted mouth, admitted, 'I bite them. It's revolting.' She looked rueful. 'I'm waiting to grow out of it.'

Her hair was fluffy and pale brown then, and now that it was no longer wet from the rain, the front part stuck out like a child's after sleep. Ever more conscious of his greedy gaze, she touched it. She asked him what he taught, and when he answered, she said, 'How fascinating', and did not sound ironic.

Michael was not entirely self-serving when he described to Katy the island where he had done his field-work. His own past had seemed to him for a long time rather dull, his experience overcropped. Events he had talked out with Viola, with friends and colleagues became again vital; he felt himself to be vigorous and fertile because a young girl was before him and was giving him her attention. Yet he was conscious of the story-teller's powers to enchant, and he put into the pell-mell fragments of his descriptions all the eloquence he could without foolishness, so that all the while, the stories he told beat out a message to her that it was he, a humdrum man with square, unprepossessing, middle-aged features, and hair going grey at the sparser temples, he who had done and seen these things, and in doing and seeing had displayed qualities of mind and imagination and courage. His experience, too, the code rapped covertly to her, was unique and subjective, not to be had except by his gift, through his eyes and his words. So he was able to love himself more.

Yet, as he talked, the Idia amongst whom he had lived in Palau would not be resigned to the role of puppets in his courtship. He conjured them and they appeared, alive, swaying in their flower-patterned sarongs, to the ring and rattle of their brass and bamboo instruments, across the fields where cloud shapes floated miles beneath in the mirroring paddies. In the core of himself, a conflagration of memory set alight for him that other beauty, perceived in Katy. Looking across at her, his blunt face flushed, he could see that she was amused, not bored.

'The children who are born with the cord around their necks become the poets,' he said. 'And they're good poets too. It's what we'd call completely arbitrary, a random selection, and it goes against all our ideas about creativity. But it works.'

'I thought children born like that died,' said Katy.

'Not always. If they survive, they're taken to the priests' house and taught the sacred texts of the tribe. These are really a history, history turned into myth, about the Idia's orgins and heroes, their wars, their conquests. Then, when they're twelve or thirteen, they have to continue writing the chronicle themselves. It's in a particular metre ...' Michael tapped on the table to show her. 'And they chant bits of it on feast days. Just like us, really, with the Old Testament.' He paused. 'Except that the Old Testament isn't really *our* story. And that theirs is never over.'

He refrained from telling Katy that he had become a part of the poem. He would another time, when she would be less likely to see in his account the boast of a man who wanted to impress her. He avoided introducing himself openly into his entertainment of her, and counted on the tension he felt in her. She would not flinch from him, but feel involved in his witness, for him and not against him. So he told her how the children who were born with the cord around their necks were set apart from all others.

'When they reach puberty, the time when they're to take up their jobs as poets' – he was keeping his idiom colloquial on purpose – 'they're taken off by a priest to a special hut, and there they're given coca leaf to chew. It acts as an anaesthetic.'

Katy nodded, and rubbed her nose. 'It goes numb,' she murmured.

Michael's eyebrows, behind his glasses, lifted a fraction, but he continued. 'Then there's a lot of praying, chanting, whatnot, and the priest operates on them.'

Katy lifted her cup to her lips, though it was empty. 'I'll get you another,' he offered.

She shook her head, impatiently. Michael could see she was beginning to jib at the length of his preamble, but he did not quicken his pace.

'He takes a special knife which they always use for ceremonies, and he dedicates it to the goddess, and dips it in her cauldron, where the coca leaves are brewing up. It's a cauldron of inspiration, and she, though a mother goddess, is also a patron of music, and presides over music, and writing, and the arts in general. She's called Dewi, and she's the source of wisdom, as well as birth.'

Michael's pleasant light voice grew confidential: 'The priest goes over to the children, who are now pretty dazed, and he makes a little cut here,' Michael took off his glasses, and pointed to the inside corner of his eye, 'down to here.' His finger travelled half-way down the side of his nose. 'And then the other side,' he pointed again. 'They remove the tear duct,' he said.

Katy's hands flew to her eye sockets and she shut her eyes

tight behind her fingers. 'Oh no,' she whispered. When she opened her eyes again, she asked, 'So they can't cry any more?'

'Just the opposite,' said Michael, bland but unable to hide his pleasure at rousing her. 'They can't stop crying. It makes them weep and weep and weep. *Your* eyes are always shining and wet because tears flow in them all the time. Not sad tears, just lubrication.' He told her that the duct is the drain of the eye, and that when it is removed the ordinary, lubricating tears have nowhere to go. 'So they pour down the poets' cheeks. Their faces become corrugated, with reddish, chapped troughs.'

Michael's own eyes glistened; they were beginning to protrude as he grew older.

'It's horrible,' said Katy. She was quite close to tears. 'Horrible.'

'I'll get you that coffee.'

Katy's hand trembled when she unwrapped the sugar lumps and put them in her coffee. Red thread veins showed in her eyes as she said, vehemently, 'It's . . . barbaric.'

'Is it? More so than all the role conditioning our society goes in for, surreptitiously?'

'That's ridiculous.' Her hands fluttered over the packet of cigarettes and then sought her bag, and patted it close to her, as if it were some comforting animal. She looked scared by her rudeness, but Michael was gratified that his words had drawn her beyond the boundaries of their brief acquaintance into a place where she could almost hiss at him. 'It's just not comparable,' she persisted, keeping her eyes down.

She was stammering, incoherently, 'Role conditioning! Yeah. I'm against the Pill, because I think, my friends think too, that it's a real hype to make girls suit what men want all over again. But it's not as bad as . . . that.' She shuddered, and lit her cigarette, fumbling.

Michael spoke with seriousness. 'You see, you're against interference, but you'd have probably liked me to interfere.

Anyway, they're stopping it now. The first missionaries who reached the Idia, in the last century, felt as you do, and they began a campaign. They covered up the women's breasts, and they stopped cock-fights, and they fought against the poets' initiation rite. There were no more ceremonies of that kind when I was last there, ten years ago. But the chroniclers were still around, and they still wept. You see, the Idia think that if the poets weep all the time, they'll use up the stock of all the sorrow in the world, the capital of grief, which is exhaustible. They turn their poets into mourners, so that others shouldn't have to mourn as well.'

Katy wavered. 'That's weird,' she said, 'weird.' But she was less fiercely opposed.

'Forgive me,' Michael said, with extreme softness, 'if I've upset you. I didn't want to. I'm sorry.'

'I'm not upset,' said Katy, with emphasis, and throwing her head back.

'If you knew the Idia,' said Michael, 'you'd find them the most civilised, artistic, fascinating people you could imagine. So far from savage, they make us look like cave-men.' He spread his hands to express his inability to convey the depths of his feeling. 'Parnassus.'

'If that was the case,' retorted Katy, 'it's probably covered with Coca Cola factories by now.'

'You can't have it both ways,' said Michael, and placed his hand flat near her arm as they went out, as if steering her past the tables and through the door, for he thought she would bridle if he touched her, if only on the sleeve of her coat.

'I'm so pleased you came,' said Michael, turning on his skates to face her for a moment. 'I thought you might not.'

'Anything rather than work.' She was harsh, but then she

looked at him for a moment openly, and muttered, 'No, I wanted to come.'

'How is work?'

'I'm still writing every essay at three in the morning. I just can't get myself sorted out to write them earlier.'

'On pills?' Michael asked, quickly.

Katy paused. 'I still don't get them finished.'

Michael caught hold of her and they stopped on the river. They were already near the fourth bridge: most of the party were behind. He forced her attention.

'You mustn't.'

'I don't do it for fun.'

She looked down and scuffed the ice surface with the spike on her toe tip.

'It makes me ill to think of it,' said Michael.

'You drink, don't you?'

'It's not the same.'

'If you weren't so shocked I might find it easier to stop. The look on your face is part of the thrill.'

'You treat me as if I were your father, or some authority figure.'

'Well you are.'

'Katy, Katy.' Michael pressed his fingers into her thin arm until he was encircling the bone, bird-like frail under her thick layers of sleeve. 'I care about you so much, please don't treat yourself so badly.'

'I don't want people to care about me.'

'Don't say such things. It's cruel, to yourself, and to . . . me.'

Katy's small, peaky face lit up with a ferociously sarcastic smile. 'Don't fuss over me,' she said, quietly. 'I can't stand it.' She shook her head. 'It bends me out of shape. Let's have a good time. It's your party.'

Katy struck out on her skates, and stumbled. Her kneecap hit the ice heavily, and she yelped at the pain. Michael dropped down beside her and put his arms around her. 'My little darling,' he murmured. Then, remembering where he was, he dropped his arms quickly to his sides and stiffly helped her to her feet. 'Are you all right now?' he asked distantly, for others had noticed her fall and were gliding up to them.

'Yes, I think so.' She rubbed her hurt knee hard, and there was surprise and a soft pleasure in her eyes that had not been present before. He squeezed her arm, avuncular.

'She's a brave girl,' he announced to the little group around her. 'No damage.'

Her look, as she registered his earlier exclamation of love and took it to her, had sent a bolt of triumph through him.

5

The boy was called Lucky, after the Lucky Strike sweatshirt that had been left behind for him by another Western observer as a tip. He raised the bamboo lattice of Michael's beach hut and said, 'Mister Lovage, tonight Ghost Dance. I dance.' He sidled under the screen and entered the small room.

'Where?' asked Michael.

'Close, close,' said Lucky. His hand ran up and down the thick bamboo bedpost, but he kept his shrewd eyes on Michael.

Michael got up and came over. His long, strong limbs seemed out of proportion in the hut, and he towered over Lucky. Knowing he was being tantalised on purpose, he smiled wryly at the boy, and asked pleadingly in Idia, 'Where?'

'No sweat,' replied Lucky. He was proud of his English. 'You listen. You go down to beach and listen. When you listen ...' Lucky's fingers rapped sharply on the hollow shaft of the post. The rhythm's resonance was muffled. 'You follow.' He added, his eyes brightening, 'Big Ghost Dance.'

Michael handed Lucky a sprig of lychee. Lucky shook his head. 'No eat before Ghost Dance,' he said.

'Of course not,' muttered Michael. 'Of course,' and shucking off the thin rough red shell, Michael bit into the tart white flesh of a berry. 'Good,' he said, with a grin.

When Lucky slipped out, barely altering the position of the screen, Michael clapped his hands over his mouth to prevent a hoot of joy, and then threw himself on his bed. He pressed his face into the lumpy straw wads in the mattress, and clenched his fists with pleasure. The night might bring fulfilment of his deepest professional ambition.

When Viola came in from the beach, Michael was still lying

there. He had not drawn the cotton bed-curtains printed with luminous waxen spirals and meanders, and she, bursting in from a bicycle ride through the coconut groves, let the light explode over his form in the screened room. Though his face was buried, the heat fell across his back and he could feel the patch of sweat on his shirt cold against his skin by contrast. He turned over, and she lay down beside him.

The blinds hung from the eaves all around; there were no fixed walls to the hut. The bed itself was a chamber, its bamboo posts held up the lashed thatch of the roof; the floor around it a verandah. Under the bed there was storage space, and at its foot stood Timmo's narrow divan. Lucky, who had taken care of the Lovages' needs since he met Michael, on a bemo ride from the capital to the sea, rented them the pavilion as lodgings on behalf of his mother; she worked in the paddies all day. It was Lucky who unearthed for Michael a work table at European height and installed it excitedly in the pavilion for him. The people of Palau wrote or painted or ate tailorwise.

Viola lay beside Michael, but she did not press her body against him. She twisted her fingers into his, and turned to look at him. They were rarely alone together, and never at night, with Timmo asleep at the foot of their bed.

'Shall I draw the bed-curtains?' she asked, flirtatious.

Michael did not kiss her. He asked, 'Where's Timmo?'

Viola answered, 'On the beach.' A moment before, Viola, with her legs stretched out, had been drifting on the langorous current of the afternoon heat. It was bearing her away to a deep heartland of pleasure. But her kind of pride prevented her moving towards Michael and acknowledging she wanted him. Michael took in her beckoning body, and instantly, her tension. But his mind was on the dance, and he felt no interest in her. She put a hand to her forehead and then, as Michael had lain before her, turned her face to the thin sheet over the knobbly mattress.

'There's a Ghost Dance tonight,' he said. 'At last!'

'Great,' murmured Viola. Unwillingly, she sounded sarcastic. 'No really, how marvellous!' she said, wiping the edge clean from her tone.

Michael knew she wanted to come with him and he flinched from the pressure of her keenness. After six weeks in Palau, he had sent Viola a telegram, asking her to join him and to bring Timmo; he had felt guilty that he did not miss them both more. When they arrived, Viola's dry ironies refreshed him after so much fervent interrogation of village elders. Her sceptical intelligence, rejecting Idia mythology as flatly as its Pythagorean astronomy, helped him. Talking to Viola, he gained distance on the material he had gathered. The tabooed sea, in which no Idia swam or fished, had seethed with ghosts one night as he walked back from the village; they crouched unseen in the dark ramparts of the waves and jeered at him in the boom of the surf. He could not bathe. The thousand acts of propitiation the Idia performed, to keep order between themselves and the spirit world, had begun to fill him with dread; at crossroads, he found himself looking for the fresh garland of frangipani on the ground before he felt secure.

But when Viola and Timmo came, they ran down to the ocean and jumped into the same menacing waves as if they were circus hoops and dragged him in alongside them.

But the bracing effect of their presence had begun to wear off, and she and Timmo had become an obligation, hampering the wholehearted conduct of his research.

'What's the dance in aid of?' Viola asked, her voice gagged by her position on the mattress.

'That young fellow, I told you.'

'To help him, is it?' said Viola, and turned over to eye her husband. Her scepticism sounded faintly hostile.

'Yes,' murmured Michael absently. He had his back to her now, and was leaning over his table on his hand. 'It'll be a long affair,' he added, warningly.

Viola disregarded this fob-off. 'I'll have a rest then,' she said, feigning a thick skin. 'And I'll ask that hippie guy to babysit.'

The north shore of the island of Palau is volcanic ash; the beaches are as fine-grained as the pink coral sand of its southern strand, but they are black. The Pacific surf leaves a scalloped edge of crystal-white foam, but against the blackness it looks like the scum of detergent on a river in Europe. These beaches are wide and desolate; the Idia's prize water, but not salt. They bathe in the freshets spouting off the volcanoes, and irrigate the rice paddies with an intricate system of conduits that spill water from terrace to terrace down the contour slopes. In these streams, fish teem so tamely that nimble-fingered children can tickle them with their hands and catch them.

On the southern shore, thickly fringed with palms, the trees arch back from the sea breeze, and when the wind blows from the land their fronds stream out like a girl's hair. But on the north shore the Pacific trades have heaped up the black sand into mountainous dunes, and these change position and shape continually. The wind strips away the matting of grass with which the Idia try to contain the erosion, and wears down the dykes they build against the encroaching sand. From one day to the next, the beach can become unfamiliar territory.

There was no moon that night, and electricity had not yet come to Palau. Michael and Viola picked their way through the pitchy dark on the soft sifting blackness of the dunes. Sea and earth mimicked each other's swelling form, but the sea heaved open with cries of rage and pain, and gashed itself along the black shore in a gasp of white blood, whilst the dunes inflated more gently and the spray that lifted in each footfall and cascaded down their shifting slopes was stealthy. The sea stormed: the sand for all its motion was pent up.

'Boo!' shouted Viola, very loudly and very suddenly.

Michael jumped. 'Blast you!' he cried.

Viola laughed. 'You're really scared!'

'Of course I am.' He took her by the arm roughly. 'I've been living with these ghosts. You're nerveless, you're not human.'

He held on to her arm, and pulled her against him. 'Now stay right beside me, and no more fun and games, all right?'

Viola's lips curved in a smile, but she let no sound escape her.

Apologetically, after a while, she spoke. 'It is spooky, I suppose.'

Michael was heavy beside her, and silent.

'But you're always telling me ...' she persisted, 'what is it? ... that spells are binding only on the consenting. Well, don't consent. I don't.'

Michael's hand on her arm pinched.

'Ow,' she said, shaking herself free.

At length Michael said, 'I hear it. It's coming from over there.' Gripping Viola's bare arm again, as if to force her to quiescent nonentity beside him, he turned his back to the ocean and struck out across the line of warm dunes. Then Viola heard it too: like the pattering of birds on a roof.

With the sea behind them, its metallic sheen and white-scarred crests no longer giving even a feeble light, the dunes' pneumatic forms enfolded Michael and Viola almost caressingly. Under their lee the air was windless, balmy. A skirling of an instrument, the beat of the drums: the sound of the dance's preparations grew clearer. Then there was a sudden clamour, as gamelan and gong were tested and struck for tone, and musicians limbered up their fingers and their wrists. Michael began walking faster. Under their feet, the warm sand became firm. He pulled Viola up by the retaining dyke and scrambled down into the palm groves on the other side. The light in the grove was sliced by the tree trunks; grey and smoothly wrinkled, like elephant hide, they glowed silvery by the light of the ritual's lamps. Viola blinked –

the lanterns' soft glimmer was dazzling after the darkness on the shore. It came driving across the trees in bright, slanting shafts. Michael started again, and Viola steadied him.

Excitement tensed his body. 'Cool it,' Viola whispered, cajoling.

The clearing in the grove was marked out by stanchions, from which hung the lanterns. The earth was beaten flat.

'I've been here before,' said Michael, surprised. 'They hold a market here sometimes.'

Viola smiled at him reassuringly. 'Ever since I came, you've told me that there's no special holy place for the Idia, that the gods are everywhere.'

'Of course.'

'Why not in a shop then? Saint Tesco's. Sounds perfect. Slightly Cornish. Perhaps a Breton missionary who came over with Tristan?'

'Viola, please.'

She wanted to tell him: your intensity terrifies me. Jocularity was her spell against him, whom she found so much more frightening than Idia ghosts.

They approached the edge of the clearing. No one paid any attention to them. Most of the crowd were squatting around two roulette wheels. On to bright baize cloths, they were tossing heaps of money, so rumpled it looked like bits of soft rag. The ball jumped and swerved through the chambers of the spinning wheel.

'They're so . . . nonchalant,' said Viola. A huge grin, like a ripe fig, burst on the betel-stained mouth of a winner. 'It's odd.'

'As we were saying,' said Michael, recovering his humour, 'the holy isn't special, it's everyday.' He told her Lucky was dancing. 'And tomorrow he'll be there with our bananas for breakfast in that old sweatshirt again.'

A group of robed priests were coming through the striped shadows of the grove into the illuminated square of the clearing.

Between them, they carried a rickety altar, made of spliced bamboo and fluttering rice paper, pink, green, lemon-yellow, with offerings of rice cakes and frangipani flowers in the centre. They set it down; there was no moment of silence, no audible beginning to the ceremony. But the babble of voices and instruments was suddenly coherent. Music rang out from the dry wooden keys of the gamelan, and whistled through the reeds of panpipes; the great bonded drums boomed, and the brass trumpet-like instrument wailed, gathering speed and increasing excitement as the mallets of the players flew through the air, invisible as the wings of humming-birds, and the fingers of the drummers, flicking the stretched skins, seemed numberless. A single sharp note sang out, and the first of the dancers jumped into the clearing. His long mask shook with bells, and he staggered under its weight of white, coarse hair, lolling tongue and wooden fangs. With legs straddling and arms raised, he took slow giant steps towards the crowd. His fingers were crowned with silver spurs, six inches long. As he approached each section of the crowd, as he scrabbled with his claws, a spectator in his line of vision fell, and with a sudden cry and closed eyes, began to follow the monster into the space.

The ring was swaying now with entranced dancers. With limbs at stiff angles and heads thrown back, they came at the huge dancing mask. He tottered and made as if to escape them, but each time rallied, and they fell away from his flashing nails. Over the frenzied drumming and rattle of the band, a hoarse cry rang out from the chattering lips of his mask. The white mane heaved.

'*PA*,' he cried, and pitched forward till the fibres swept the beaten earth.

'*GE!*' He raised himself, and shuddered, till the jaw of the mask clattered furiously and the blooded tongue shook. His curse twisted through the locks of the huge wig and set all the clappers of the bells clacking.

43

'*LA*,' he groaned. Jerking himself to his tiptoes, and hurling back his burdened head, he shouted the final imprecation at his assailants. '*RAU*.'

'*Pagelarau*,' whispered Michael. 'You are bewitched.'

Lucky passed in front of them. His eyes were open but he made no sign of recognition. His bare chest was soaked in sweat and his ribs stood out. He stamped and shuffled, bending over to trail on the ground the curved sword he was carrying, as if its weight was overpowering him. His glistening back as he twisted away from them was hard as stone. Slowly he turned with the other dancers and began to move, with a wading motion, towards the figure in the mask. Slowly, as if every ounce of strength were altogether necessary, the sword dancers lifted their weapons and began to take aim. Slowly, they drove their swords towards the figure in the mask, the sorcerer.

Viola between parted fingers cried, 'No!'

Michael said, in her ear, 'Watch, silly.'

She watched. A single, splitting high note screamed from the orchestra. As it vibrated in the clearing, the swords fell limply in their grasp, before they had even touched him.

As if on a spring, the body of the masked man leapt clean into the air, all bells jangling, the huge red agape mouth snapping to his wild jerks.

The dancers fell back. Many crawled on the ground, dragging their limbs. The orchestra, at full strength now, took up the syncopated rhythm of the mask with drum and cymbal, pipe and gamelan.

Viola dropped her hands from her face; but her tension was not eased by the dinning music. She watched Lucky crawl and then the sword he was carrying lift itself, as if of its own volition, to turn gracefully upwards and round until its point was driving at Lucky's face. All around him, the dancers' weaving figures struggled against their weapons; one by one they failed, and turned their swords against themselves. Michael's eyes, avid for more, were lit up, almost cheekily.

Viola looked, hardly daring to look. She saw the point of the sword in Lucky's cheek probe the flesh into a cavity; his jaw was set and sweat streamed down his face. His whole frame, rigid with tensed muscle, gibbered and shook. But the sword did not pierce his flesh. As the dancers around him thrashed to repulse the evil that assailed them, the mask uttered another harsh cry. One by one, they collapsed, their swords falling from their inert arms. With puzzled eyes, they began to look around them at the spectators, and slowly pulled themselves up and shuffled back into the crowd.

On the edge of the clearing, one young, slim figure remained, curved over the kris as if cradling it. His eyes were closed, and he trembled all over, locked in a self-wounding trance. The mask clattered nearer and nearer to him, herding him towards the altar. The principal priest approached this last remaining dancer, and forced his dreaming head into a bowl of liquid. His teeth were chattering so, he had difficulty drinking. The priest tilted back his head, and tipped the cup between his lips. The man swallowed, and suddenly, wrenching himself free from the priest's hold, spat out the liquid on the ground and vomited. The violence shook him out of his trance, and he screamed. Then tears fell down his cheeks, his shivering became stilled. The priest patted him on the back.

'*Madempanou*, you will be free,' muttered Michael, moving his lips with the priest.

Viola tugged at Michael's arm to take him away. He stopped her. 'He named the witch!' he said. 'The one who's put him in that state.'

You scare me, she wanted to say. 'I can't take any more.'

'Go back then.'

How can I? Viola almost moaned. (Black dunes, black beach, the darkness.)

From the ranks of the crowd a girl was being pushed forward. Her eyes fell on the youth standing by the priest, and fear mixed with tenderness caused a spasm on her face before she recovered her composure and walked with swaying grace towards the altar.

6

In Michael's rooms in college, there was a door which Katy had never seen him open. Another led to a second room he could use as a bedroom if he chose; but the first door seemed false, an ornament to maintain symmetry in the seventeenth-century wainscoting.

They had been looking at Michael's photographs of Palau. He kept them in plastic sleeves, and they were holding them up against the light of his deeply mullioned windows. Outside, across the lawn, there was an old magnolia tree, standing alone against the smooth expanse of the college chapel's perpendicular stone wall, and its dark, glossy leaves cut across the geometrical tracery of the window and scrambled the images in front of her eyes.

Michael said, 'I'll give you a slide show another time. But it takes so long.'

She did not respond. Instead, she asked him about the door.

'It just leads to a store,' he said and, getting up, opened it.

The room had no window. He found the switch and turned on the central hanging light; the lampshade was of parchment that had cracked with age. Katy joined Michael at the jamb.

'Books!' she exclaimed.

'I bought a colleague's library when he died. He died intestate, and there were lots of outstanding bills for his widow.' Michael sighed. 'I must get round to sorting them. It's an excellent collection.'

Katy entered the room. She passed through a gap between the stacked wine cartons filled with books, and turned around to survey the heap from the other end of the room. 'There must be thousands of books here!'

'Just about a thousand, I think. I was very lucky to get them. They were going cheap, the dealers couldn't be bothered to itemise them.'

Katy approached one pile of three cases and opened the tucked flaps.

'He specialised in the Pacific, like me.'

'*Trance-Dancing in Bali*,' Katy read. She picked it up.

'Good, I'll bring that in. Thanks.' He held out his hand to receive the book, but Katy was looking at it.

There was a photograph of a child, her face bleached white with powder, and a golden pin decorated with blossom in her piled hair. Her body, swaddled in gilded bands, was a narrow pipe, and above it she extended her fragile and slender arms with forlorn rigidity, as if they were carved out of jade and she were the trunk of an ornamental tree. Her small hands flowered into adroit and formal gestures. She was loaded with bracelets; some hung in fetters on her ankles above her bare, splayed feet. Her eyes were closed, her lips parted; beside her, three men sitting cross-legged on a dais beat on instruments that resembled xylophones. Their mallets were blurred from the speed of the rhythm they beat out to accompany her dancing.

Katy leafed on. Another photograph: in a clearing ringed by spectators, some in turbans, all in sarongs, the women's nurturant breasts uncovered, an old woman danced. She was unadorned, and her body was spectre-like in its ribbed thinness. Her breasts, by contrast to the younger women's, hung like dried fruits on either side of her ridged breastbone. Her face, flung back as she bent her emaciated body to the music, wore an expression of serene, sightless rapture.

Michael moved and stood behind Katy's shoulder. 'She's prophesying.'

'What?'

'Usually vague: fertility, a rich harvest, nothing too precise.'

'And the child?' Katy leafed back.

'No, children don't prophesy. They dance to exorcise evil; their beauty is meant to be … prophylactic.' He thought: but the innocent are the most vulnerable to attack. From evil spirits as well as good. It is the young who are witches. He did not speak his thoughts aloud.

Katy was looking at him, inquiringly. He still did not want to tell her what he was thinking. 'Prophylactic? What's that?' she asked eventually. She prided herself on not pretending to knowledge she did not have.

'A remedy, a prevention, a barrier. Like a contraceptive. The child dancing puts her goodness between the people for whom she dances and the spirits that might attack them. And the evil they ascribe to her, that too protects them from it.'

'Does it work?'

Michael laughed, emptily.

How Viola had screamed at him when the witch wouldn't eat. *That girl is dying and you are doing nothing.* He spoke aloud: 'Do you think it could? Do you believe in evil?'

'I suppose not.'

It does work, actually. It works very effectively indeed. After a ritual dance the village feels cleansed, serene, set up for another spell of life. It's a kind of birth ceremony. They have similar ceremonies in my island, in Palau.'

'We have to get nearer!' Michael edged his way from the front of the crowd and, pulling Viola behind him, threaded his way round the back to a vantage point just behind the chief priest himself. The gamelan orchestra on the priest's left was swinging through a gentle rhythm, marking time, exchanging smiles as they riffed languidly through the interval. The stain in front of the priest's feet on the ground was reddish. There were streaks of brownish yellow in it, like banana. The exorcised youth wiped the tears from his cheeks with the fallen end of his turban right across his nose and face with the clumsy gesture of a child. He looked up and across the clearing, with longing and urgency in his eyes. They widened suddenly when he met her quick look, before he averted his gaze again.

The young girl was walking alone with a cluster of men and women at her back. She was barefoot and turbanned; gold hoops in her ears danced as she walked towards the youth and the altar with the graceful, easy sway of the Idia water-carrying women-folk. Behind her, just keeping their distance, the crowd of men and women stared silently. She stopped, and when she did, they all stopped too, so that the people at the back stumbled and cried out in irritable fear. As she turned her head to look at them, there was infinite insolence in her gaze.

Then she continued to cross the clearing. Like stalkers, they pressed behind her again, until she stood in front of the priest and the boy. The spectators pushed up, filling the space where the Ghost Dance had taken place but leaving a protective circle of a few feet around her. From the orchestra, now barred from view by the crowd, came soft whispers and low trills and the steady susurrus of a snare vibrating on a drum.

Michael switched on his tape-recorder.

The victim of witchcraft shrank away behind the shoulder of the priest. Her look followed him, and when she caught his eyes, the contemptuousness of her full lips softened. Though her mouth did not move, she seemed to smile at him almost maternally. 'It is not my fault you are bewitched,' she said. 'But only on my account.'

The priest rebuked her, spitting words at her with rapid anger. She stared past his head, unresponsive. Her unseeing gaze passed over Michael, and thrilled through him. The girl did not reply to the priest. The priest barked again, demanding a full confession of her sorceries. Her eyes came back and held the priest at the level of his chest. She could not bear to look into his face. To his chest, she said, softly and with a tone of resignation, 'I am not to blame.' She lifted a hand and waved it over her own body, from her feet to her head. 'This my form', she said with the same soft hopelessness, 'is the god's habitation and his making.'

The youth behind the priest covered his face; sobs began to shake him. The assistant priest gave him a sharp jab in the ribs and shouted something angrily in his ear.

The chief priest said, 'You have enchanted him.'

'Yes,' she said, 'he is enchanted. But I am not responsible.'

'The god spoke, through the Dance.'

Then her mouth twisted with vulgar looseness for an instant, and she looked up quickly sideways at the priests, and said, 'Besides, you have cured him now.'

The chief priest snapped erect and tossed his head. 'Take her away,' he ordered.

'Yes, take me away,' she said, wearily, and turned on her heel.

The crowd fell away from her. Suddenly, she stopped and looked back. 'Ketut,' she spoke out the boy's name, 'Ketut, have I really bewitched you?'

'*Pagelanam*,' he moaned. The priest signalled to his companion, and he walked the youth away.

'You are cured now,' the priest commanded him.

'Yes, I am cured,' Michael heard the boy moan, and again he passed the grimy end of his turban across his face like a snuffly nosed child.

'Could we do something like that here, in England?'

'Trance-dance?'

Katy closed her eyes. 'Yes, and be strong and clean and new. Be lost to everything for a time, like that old woman.'

'You need belief. We once had it, but I'm not sure it's a good thing.'

Katy opened her eyes. 'I think we need it back again.'

'Unfortunately, it's quite easy to bring it back. I always say, spells are binding only on the consenting. Witchcraft between consenting adults, you might say.'

Katy put the book in his hand. He took her wrist and asked if he might kiss her. She said nothing. The question shot through her like a quick burning fuse. She did not move, and in her stillness there was consent. So he lifted her up on to a pile of book-filled cartons and caressed her fiercely without taking off her clothes until the smell of staleness, dust and printed paper in the storeroom was entirely altered and transfused by her musk.

Katy was eighteen. After the first encounter in the bookroom, she determined that this time she would do as she was done by, and not let herself be played upon but return his caresses. But she was checked by the character of Michael's desire. Once, when she moved a hand towards his waistband, to undo the buckle of his belt, he took her hand gently and said, 'No.' She could not insist. She was baffled by the incompleteness of his needs, and was shy of asserting herself. Yet what she saw as her selfishness in their love-making bothered and upset her. When once she began to say, 'Don't you want to come?' he interrupted quickly, and said, 'It makes me happy to make you happy, and you are, aren't you, little one?' And so she was made infantile, though he called her his queen too, and liked to lift her to sit above him, his mouth between her legs. But she, licked and caressed till she moaned, was still a nursling. Only once did she get the better of his will, and he went into her and came. But afterwards he was angry; he wanted always to remain in control. She was offended. They quarrelled.

'If you didn't want to that much, you shouldn't have,' she cried. She hated his remorse.

'But I'm twenty years older than you, even more,' he groaned.

'But I don't understand, what's the difference between . . .' she faltered.

'I know, I know, it's stupid. Forgive me. But I love you and it seems so wrong. What can I give you? Nothing.'

'But I don't want anything,' she said. 'What could I want?'

'We can't be lovers, not completely. I'm happy the way we are.' He held her chin up towards him and scrutinised her peaky smudged face. 'You satisfy me completely, don't you see.'

But Katy wanted Michael to be moved, as deeply as he moved her with his hands and with his tongue, and resentment of his impassivity grew inside her.

7

Jimmy held on to Viola's arm; she took his weight without constraint.

'I think he's a dish,' she said, nodding in the direction of Andrew.

Jimmy's eyes wandered and landed, with obvious vacant concentration, on a black alder up to its waist in the river. He answered: 'There are some moments when life seems to come together, to be solved, rather in the same way as in my line, though I can tackle a problem step by step, through the records, the newspapers ... I'd rather get the feel of a period in an instinctual way through its rhythm, its flow, its spirit. That's why I read so much fiction. Frowned on harshly by my fellow-historians. But, but – '

'The immanent spirit,' said Viola. 'The Chinese painters tried to set it down on paper too. Ch'i. Grasped through contemplation. It goes through the nerves, bypassing the brain.'

'Yes, something like that. I can have a set of facts and figures in front of me that have to be made to make sense; or at least, the lack of sense they make has to be understood. It's usually that way round! I can just let it lie inside me, leavening, to use the image of the good book. That method works far far better than toiling away. Suddenly, overnight, the idea has risen, the notes are no longer a mass of disconnected fragments, but a coherent body, coalesced. Bread!' Jimmy gestured, bringing the fingertips of both hands together to form a sphere and pitching forward.

Viola clutched him, and he laughed. 'That's how it was the day I met him again.' His eyes travelled to Andrew, skating beside Timmo. 'All day, I'd been completely ... possessed ... by coherence. It felt like ... a blessing. Really. I walked out of college in the morning, to have a coffee at Spider's, and as I passed the window of Manderson's I saw a picture that I immediately liked, liked enormously. It wasn't signed but I found out later – I'll come to that – that it was an early Mondrian. You would never have recognised it, not even you, Viola. It was a tender, flowing kind of drawing with chalks, with a naked boy, a faun-like boy, just the type I like, with a high bottom and curls on his head ...' Jimmy gestured, his bespectacled, red-nosed, blunt-faced respectability suddenly dainty in imitation, '... with flowers, rather Redon-like, peonies, chrysanthemums, big, generous open flowers, all massed around him. You couldn't quite tell the planes: the flowers weren't in a vase, or a garland, they were a kind of symbolic extension of the boy, who was cherry-ripe, my dear, not a fawn in the other sense at all. I thought how much I should like to have it, and then dismissed the thought from my mind as impossible. Except that I promised myself, should any windfall come my way, I'd inquire about its price. I'm not leaning too hard on you?'

'I think you're getting the hang of the movement, aren't you?' said Viola.

'I can't concentrate on it. I'd rather talk to you.'

'So I see.' Viola smiled at him, and gave his arm a squeeze. 'I *am* listening.' They both looked at Timmo and Andrew's efforts just ahead of them, and then at each other again, reassured.

'I had my coffee. It was hot. It was good. Spider's can be so unreliable.'

'I know.'

'When I got back to my rooms, the telephone was ringing. It was Jerome Namier, calling from New York.'

Viola nodded. '*The Critical Review*, I know. His new, hugely rich, oil-financed art mag.'

'That's it. "Jimmy," he said in that stammering way that he has, like a message in Morse code, "Jimmy, I know it's a te-te-terrible, fri-fri-frightful, gha-gha-ghastly nuisance" (and I think his accent has got even plummier since he crossed the Atlantic) "but I thought you might enjoy, just might enjoy", and so forth.' Jimmy's small, slightly watery eyes gleamed behind his glasses as he imitated the editor. 'The upshot is that he wanted a review of a recent study in my field: a new book about the economics of prostitution, some structuralist's breakdown, eight hundred pages long, you know the sort of thing.'

'And he pays well, so back you went to the Mondrian?'

'It wasn't a *real* Mondrian. At Manderson's? Hardly. It was a fine quality print.'

'I never knew he'd been a figure painter at all.'

'You must come and see it ... But to continue with the saga of my perfect day, the moment when Andrew would say my stars were right ...' Again his eyes sought out Andrew's figure, drawing ahead of them.

'It's great you're happy.'

'Yes, isn't it?' Jimmy sighed.

'Don't sigh.'

'How long will it last, I ask myself?'

They were passing under a wooden, humpbacked footbridge, linking the college on their left with the river's southern bank. Viola put her hand up to the fringe of icicles that hung from the dark, glistening underside of the arch, and looked at the drops of dew that appeared on her warm gloves as the frost dissolved at contact with them. How instant the response of ice is to the touch, she thought. She broke off an icicle. It came away with a neat, sharp snap; she poked it into her hand. Its point passed cleanly through the knitted fabric; she withdrew it, and threatened Jimmy, waving it near his face. He flinched away, laughing. Viola continued to hold it, but it melted wet and cold in her grasp, so she tossed it aside. It fell on the river with a tinkle.

'Carry on. I am interested. I really am. I'd like to know how it happens, this perfect day.'

'I had to go up to London. I took the train. When I came out of the tube station at Piccadilly, I bought some newsrag, for the gossip. Always *so* thrilling! And I heard above my head the sound of a shackle. It struck a hollow bar of the scaffolding. I looked up, I suppose I was scared it might fall. And there was this unmistakable bottom, this sublime derrière.'

'You're shocking.' Viola was giggling.

Jimmy was serious. 'Come now. It'd be more shocking if I didn't know them again, now, wouldn't it?'

Viola smiled. 'How do you know when you don't know them again? You can't.'

'Stop it. I do know them again. And in this case, it wasn't just a case of recognition. I felt this kind of surge . . .'

'Don't be filthy.'

'No, it's much more romantic than sex.'

Viola interrupted, 'That's a real homosexual's remark. To us heteros, there's nothing more romantic than sex.'

'Listen, it was a kind of heat flowing through me, kind of . . . annealing me. It was that feeling of coherence again. Andrew's generation call it a "rush". Good word for it. He was up there carrying a huge neon letter G. He was connecting it. I watched him move until my neck ached. Then he came down the ladder that led from one level of the scaffolding to another, and reached the pavement. I didn't move. I just stood there. But it was a special day, and he came straight over to me as if no time had elapsed since our last encounter. He said, "I was just thinking about you".' Jimmy paused, slightly breathless, 'You can imagine the rest.'

'I don't know that I can,' said Viola. 'Besides, I'm not sure I want to.' She paused. 'It's amazing it hasn't worn off. What do you talk to him about? The economics of prostitution?' She realised her clumsiness too late. 'I'm sorry,' she held on to his arm. 'It just came out.'

'Viola, I should think I know by now that to be friends with you means putting up with your tongue.' Jimmy was stiff, his eyes distant.

Love never leaves one at a loss for things to talk about, she remembered. It charges all experience, it inspires a stream of questions about the beloved, it's a constant process of mutual inquiry, it changes the humdrum or the neutral exchanges. It's a language of its own, altering the usual meaning of language in current use. She saw Michael in front of them, exuberant, gesturing, beside the thin student. With a pang so sharp that she pulled her arm away from Jimmy to hold herself steady, Viola turned her mind to the knowledge of the child she had once incorporated, made one with herself during his gestation and birth and nurture. She lifted her head to watch Timmo, and her wonder was so complete it washed away all the cynicism and amusement with which she had listened to Jimmy. She considered Timmo's being, and marvelled that the feeling in the end of her nipples when he had cried for milk as a baby was still so acutely remembered by her body that it did not in fact belong to memory – that museum – but to the living present. She recalled how in the company of Timmo as a child, the anguish of communication was exiled, the problem of what to say never occurred.

As if echoing her, Jimmy said slowly, 'So far that hasn't been a problem. There are other things besides talk.' He assumed an expression of mock wickedness, but his effort was spoiled by his evident, vulnerable tenderness. 'He's a good boy – wild, a bit exotic, like so many of the young these days, almost a foreigner in the England I was brought up in.' He tugged at her elbow to stop, and said with unusual earnestness, 'They've a different experience of life, they've learned to set it at a much lower price. Post-war plenty has reared them in a kind of brutality. It's shocking, it's a shocking upset of all the illusions that men like Michael still fight for. But this brutality's shaped them. I can amaze Andrew far more profoundly by reading a book fast, say in a morning, than I can by boasting about some sexual adventure. At nineteen, he's used to such behaviour, or to use an old-fashioned term, to such depravity, that even a seasoned cottage queen like myself can't spring any surprises.'

'I'm not sure I want you to go on,' Viola interrupted. 'I think of what Timmo might know too, and it scares me.' She had a certain appetite for Jimmy's notorious outspokenness, but it had its limits.

'The fascinating thing is how he and others like him keep their innocence. He calls it being streetwise, and it seems to me that it means knowing everything there is to know so that you can't get caught unawares. It's the opposite of the old innocence, the kind that was the equivalent of ignorance ...'

Viola nodded, 'Yes, like not teaching girls to read and write because then they couldn't conduct clandestine love affairs.'

'Yes, exactly. But Andrew and his kind are looking for a total knowledge of possible evil; for them, not getting "fazed" is a kind of armour that keeps them, well, pure. For want of a better word. In fact, he's not really homosexual at all. To use his own jargon, he'll just try anything. Then nothing, he figures, will get to him.'

Viola looked around as Andrew and Timmo overtook. They waved and dashed ahead. Andrew was talking to Timmo, laughing and gesticulating. He was a pale, very pale youth, with the pallor of a bad diet and small hours; his face was flattish, nose and forehead running in a smooth line as on a visor, his eyes with their heavy, almost swollen lids were set wide apart and added to the Slavic cut of his features. But the total effect was candid, sleepy, disarming; beside him, Timmo, with his disturbing crookedness of feature, seemed almost more knowing. She signalled to Jimmy to set off again after them.

Viola knew Jimmy had first met Andrew at a sauna bath. The meeting had been the subject of a long and salacious exposition of the gay life that Viola had found compelling and repellent at once. She did not know what the interior of such a place might be like. The only sauna she herself had ever taken was with Michael in a log cabin in the Connecticut woods. One of his anthropologist colleagues from Columbia had built it in the grounds of his country retreat, and one evening Viola and Michael joined the whole family for their daily bath. It had been a radiant summer's day, and the sunlight, even under the dappling canopy of golden maples, was so brilliant that her vision had turned black at the edges, as if burned by the dazzle; the heat, like a bear hug, had crushed the wind out of her heart if she walked at more than a gentle amble, and the humidity clung like muslin. But at twilight, which fell late – it was soon after the solstice – the heat was pleasant and the family led Viola and Michael to the hut in the woods, and there, very shyly, Viola took off all her clothes and intertwined herself with the hot soft bodies of their friend's wriggling children on the slatted benches.

It was very dark inside the hut; the wooden walls streamed with moisture, the steam from the sizzling coals rose in sharp exhalations when their hosts threw water on them and caught in her throat so that she had to clutch a wet flannel to her mouth to get her breath back. Her heart began to beat faster and faster, with a heavy thump, and when she opened her eyes, her eyeballs felt seared by the tremendous temperature. She fell back against the wooden seat, with the children gasping and laughing around her. She saw the brown, smooth, well-fed body of their friend, and the generous, slippery fleshiness of his wife, and on the other side of them, Michael's thin hairy legs and thin smooth chest and long hairy arms. Vanity about her own physical presence beside them naked in the hut became impossible, and she enjoyed this ebbing of the narcissism called shame, and she wanted Michael to want her. She saw now Jimmy and Andrew joining them and the sprawling children in the dark, hot vapours of the hut; she saw them sitting up, unvanquished by the inertia she and her friends felt; impervious to inhibition and alert to desire. In the gloom their faces were grotesquely shadowed, the light from the glowing coal played on their features, the steam threw into relief the hollows of their eyes, the flare of their nostrils, the blackness of the hole their mouths made; Jimmy without his glasses looked undressed, and his bland words, 'I caught his eye, he caught mine, that's how it happened. I went over to him', became obscene. Viola envied them.

She shut her eyes tight, and then opened them. She was relieved to see Jimmy's mild, bespectacled, and modest face beside her, and she pressed her hand on his arm.

'You mustn't tell me too much,' she said. 'It gets to me sometimes. You forget how squeamish we straights can be.'

'Michael behaving?' asked Jimmy.

'Why? Do you think he isn't?'

'I can never tell about you two.' Then he added, 'And work?'

Viola blew on her hands through her gloves. 'I'm so glad you want to know!' She smiled at him. 'You're a real friend, you know.' And she began telling him how the aesthetic qualities of a painting are themselves altered by extrinsic factors that have nothing to do with the way the picture looks. 'If you learn that the blue used by Lorenzetti for the Madonna and Child in a certain church in Siena was solid lapis lazuli specially ordered from Constantinople and that it cost the Podestà X hundred gold pieces in exchange, which they raised in a special tax, it does rather change your appreciation of those utterly stiff, striated draperies, doesn't it? I mean the cost and the effort makes a difference to how you appreciate the blanket use of the blue: it's no longer a rather repetitive vehicle to express the contours of the Virgin's body, and in fact failing to do that. It's a bill, it's like coins round the neck of an Orubu girl.'

Viola took Jimmy's arm. She was a bit out of breath, but she went on chattering to him with her usual vivacity, about how she was working on the interpretation of some frescoes, and how they fitted in with her work in the field to date. She talked, and Jimmy listened, with half an ear. She had told him some of it before, but it was comforting, between friends, to be able to repeat oneself and carry on talking as, still holding on to Jimmy, she passed the cluster of people who had gathered around the white-faced girl when she fell for an instant on the ice.

8

'I helped with the lights at Crack's last gig. It was a good break.'
Andrew was cold; he spoke with stiff lips. He watched Jimmy
skating ahead with Viola.

'Let's get moving,' said Timmo. 'This is getting to be like hard
work.' He paused. 'Crack aren't bad.

> 'Don't love my mum!
> Don't love my dad!
> Don't love my brother!
> I get off on hate!'

Timmo hummed and attempted to stomp, legs and arms at
right angles, shoulders raised on either side of his jerking head.
He slithered and laughed. 'What's the group like?'

'They haven't got your upmarket accent, for one thing.'

Timmo grimaced.

'They're crazy. No, that's not right. They're dead ordinary.'

'They're pissed off.'

'Yeah.'

'I don't go for that. Nothing pisses me off more than being
pissed off.'

Andrew went on, 'I was at school with Pete, Pete Razorblade,
now, that was Pete Simpson. He's a good musician, always was.
Sang the lead tenor in the school choir. "And shall we build
Jerusalem,/In England's green and pleasant land?"' Andrew
piped in imitation. 'Just like that, with a fucking prune in his
mouth. We used to hang around outside the pub while our mums
and dads were knocking it back inside . . . when I first met Crack,
I saw the guys coming in, and then Ice Lolly, the drummer.

I said, "Where's Poppy?" She's the real stuff, just *great* on guitar. Someone said, "She's bringing the gear." And in comes Poppy Sickle, dragging God knows what. Amplifiers, suitcases, mikes. Crazy. And she's meant to be looking after her hands.'

Talking was warming Andrew up; he was moving more easily now.

Timmo had seen Crack's last record, Neutron, which sold well after the papers raised hell about its obscenity. The sleeve showed Pete Razorblade in a tulle tutu over shredded jeans and cowboy boots, flinging his starveling arms and legs into cryptic angles, while beside him Ice Lolly posed in cropped hair and streaked face as a victim of the bomb. The other two members of the group lay on the ground, in grainy black and white, like corpses in a war photograph. The music was anchored to a beat as regular as a derrick, and above it, Pete Razorblade's voice fluted and warbled in a frenzied impersonation of a castrato singer. Timmo listened to their rage and it excited him; just like the ogres and vile crones and merciless enchantresses of fairy stories in the first books of his reading life, they enacted his dreamed perversion and malignancy and filled him with satisfaction. Michael, hearing them play, would show his scorn, and Timmo, aware that his father did not understand his sense of separateness, provoked his anger by play-acting identification with the band. 'Fuck me, this soup is hot,' he'd say callously, and then glaze his features into the simulacrum of total innocence when his father began to quake with fury.

'Do they really have all those fights?' he asked Andrew.

'Poppy and Ice Lolly love to think they're really mean and really tough. Last time, Ice Lolly came up to me after the gig, she put her hand on my flies, you know, squaring her shoulders, and giving me the eye. She said, real slow, "Well, where is it then?"' Andrew turned his face to Timmo, and imitated the girl's scorn. 'Well, I laughed. A sort of really nervous, high laugh. The kind that isn't a laugh at all. But she didn't laugh back. She's a real performer.'

Timmo said, 'Tough.' He raised his eyebrows, then frowned. They caught up with Jimmy and Viola, and smiled, overtaking with a happy competence.

'The spooky thing is', Andrew went on, 'it's a part she's playing. It's the one she knows best and she can't get away from it. Afterwards, when we'd got everything in the van, and it was three in the morning, she flopped down beside Poppy and put her head in Poppy's lap, and began to cry, real big wet tears, and Poppy began to bawl with her, and in the end they're hugging each other like two kids, and then all that yuck they wear on their face gets into their eyes and they start yelping and wiping it into ucky smears all over everything. Then they fall asleep, bang.' He paused, 'I fancied her rotten, too.'

Timmo laughed, 'Heavy!'

Andrew paused. 'Pete'd die laughing if he saw me here with Jimmy and that lot, your old man, so straight. But they're all getting their rocks off, aren't they, and no grief.'

Timmo said dully, 'Don't know.' He looked at Andrew. 'Do your mother and father still have it off?' He could not help but sound stilted.

'Oh yeah,' said Andrew. 'I can always tell. Dad, looks, well, kind of puffed up, like a pigeon, when he's had his end away, and Mum larks about at breakfast. But it's not often.' Andrew added, when Timmo did not speak, 'And your folks?'

Timmo shook his head. 'I just don't know.'

'She's a good-looker, your mum.'

Timmo was silent. Andrew was about four years his elder, he guessed. He seemed so . . . knowledgeable, Timmo felt stifled by envy and ignorance. He was too proud to admit his own in-experience, and yet he wanted to talk about himself and his lack of opportunity to experience what seemed Andrew's common-place world. It was as if his father had inverted the fertility magic he wrote about, and the gabled, tree-sheltered farm at Hartbridge stood unpeopled by the spirits of congress and desire.

Timmo recalled one sequence Michael had made for a television film about Palau. It had begun in darkness; only the bulk of the high and bulbous stupas loomed darker against the pre-dawn sky. Then, as if a moving finger were describing the dividing line of earth and air, the light of the rising sun shot through the darkness, and began to seep upwards and turn the valleys and folds below the island's central volcano into the tender rose grey of an oyster, against which, isolated and filled with menace, the black stupas stood like vigilantes on a ridge. When the sun itself exploded out of the sea, all the tender mistiness vanished and a golden cataract of light cut the landscape forms into hard contours; gradually the relief sculptures on the temple emerged with all their grinning and grimacing concatenations of divinities. But the temple itself remained bleak even in the sunburst.

Then Michael had walked into the frame, casually appearing from behind one of the sacred pillars as if strolling about in his own front garden, and explained that this was the most holy place in the whole of Palau, the mother temple of the highest god – Timmo could not remember his name – and that the god only visited his temple on his feast day. The rest of the year he lived elsewhere, and no rites were carried out. The altars and stupas stood abandoned, as now.

It had been curious for Timmo to feel so affected by the desolation left behind by a god in whom he did not, could not believe. Yet he was, just as he felt uncomfortable, even throttled, when his mother took him into Italian churches on their trips abroad together, and he was confronted by the opposite of Palau, by a church with a loyal god who is daily attended by his votaries.

His father, breezy, agnostic, standing there spouting in the sinister emptiness left by the peripatetic god, had remained in his son's memory, and the menacing sanctuary around Michael became a template to him of his own home, for it too had been vacated by the spirits that animate and desire. Timmo had wanted the temple to be thronged with wild, waving, shouting, dancing people, while instead there was only this cheery British trespasser, his father.

'Does your mother ever make out with anyone?'

Timmo shrugged his shoulders. 'How would I know?'

He thought he was going to cry and he shook himself furiously, narrowing his eyes as he looked across the screen of white alders, to the fields where the frost still sparkled under the northerly hedgerows but had melted under the sun off the trees' bright, wet branches.

Professor Wilton glided up on Timmo's other side. His body moved with the stately smoothness of a finely calibrated engine, holding his hands clasped together behind his back. His pink face, framed by his white hair, glowed with pleasure in his own gracefulness. The boys were stumblers by comparison.

'Well, Timothy, my young friend, how are you?'

Timmo smiled; the crossness between his brows softened. 'I'm well, thank you. And you?'

'Good, good,' said the old man, ignoring the question. 'And how are Limits?' He looked amused.

'I'm still adding to them. I've found some astronomical examples . . .' He stammered, and then began again. 'Examples from astronomy, I mean.' His manner with Wilton was respectful, and his voice dropped instantly the blunting of the vowels and tonguing of the consonants he'd assumed when alone with Andrew.

'Good, good,' said Wilton again. 'It's coming along then? Should have a look at computers, try that, I would. Too old myself for them now. But interesting things.'

Timmo, in loyalty to the excluded Andrew, turned to him. 'Last time Professor Wilton and I met, I told him I was writing down the limits of things . . .'

'What things?'

'Professor Wilton knows,' Timmo hesitated, '*all* about what people used to think. About why the world was flat and the stars were fixed.'

'But I'll have to keep up with you to remain up-to-date now.'

Timmo put his head sideways, pleased at the old man's chaffing, and went on, looking again at Andrew, and gesticulating with sudden quick eagerness. 'One book's called *The Column and the Flea's Knee*, and it's about the invention of the column and the flea's jump. A flea jumps higher than, oh, a hundred times higher than itself. It's about strain, and tension, and how people overcame it, or used it, like in suspension bridges. It's about why we can stand on this ice today and not fall through it.'

Wilton said, 'And young Timothy here, last time we met, was set on working out exactly how thin the ice could be before we fell through.' Wilton laughed again. 'As it were. He was tabulating his findings to provide . . .' He waved at the glittering scene of white sun and ice all around them,' 'a complete formula for the very nature of space. That's it, isn't it?'

'You know that's not possible,' Timmo murmured. He was flattered by the old man's attention.

'I heard down in London that universities were up to here with fruitcakes.' Andrew was trying to be light.

'Not a fruitcake, not at all.' Wilton tapped his head. 'Oh no.'

Timmo continued, hardly listening, 'Hey, Andrew, you could probably give me the limits on your lights. What I'm aiming at is this. If you sing A you can sing it between such and such a number of frequencies, and it'll sound, to the ordinary human ear, like A. But there are limits, and at some point – I'm not talking about perfect pitch or child prodigies – it'll start sounding flat, or sharp. A above Middle C is such a vibration, that's what piano tuners know and there are limits to it, on either side, measurable in the frequency. Now with your lights, I imagine that if you intensify a certain neon tube, say yellow, it'll stay yellow within certain points. Beyond that, it'll turn white, or orange, or something.'

Andrew nodded. 'Yeah. The tubes heat up and change colour.'

'That's it!' Timmo waved his hands about. 'Maybe the relation of heat to colour can be measured! Maybe red neon has definable limits!'

Wilton smiled, indulgent. 'And you'll set it down. A new secular Bible. Crammed with truths.'

Timmo continued to address Andrew, passionately. All his earlier affectation of hangloose, sulky impassiveness was gone. 'Listen, Andrew, Professor Wilton's teasing me. Of course he should tease. But there are only five regular forms that can exist in space. He wrote that in his book, and it blew my mind, honest, when I read it. It's not just our minds that are limited, but space itself is. You just can't get beyond the cube, the pyramid, what's it, the tetrahedron, the two polyhedrons . . . okay, okay.' Andrew was spreading his hands.

Timmo dropped on his haunches on the ice. He began scratching at the surface with his thumb nail, drawing a form composed of twenty regular triangles, and then, with equal impatience, and disregard of the shards splintering under his fingernail, the twelve five-sided pentagons of the other regular polyhedron.

'And that's what?' Andrew scuffed the sketch with the point of his skate.

'A dodecahedron. But the point is, not the word, but the fact that it's one of only five forms with regular faces that have ever existed or will ever exist in this universe.' Timmo was rushing his words pell-mell, and as he stood up, he took a deep breath, looked at Wilton and said, 'And that to me is the best thing since sliced bread.'

'Sliced bread is yuck,' said Andrew.

Timmo would not be subdued, and he came back at him quickly. 'Listen to this, then.' He paused. 'Seventy is about the average life span, right?'

Andrew nodded. 'Given you don't do anything I would do.'

'Apart from that, wise guy.'

'Okay.'

'In seventy years, a man's heart beats about twenty-five million times.'

'You're the one who knows.'

'And how many times do you suppose a rabbit's heart beats in the seven years of its normal life?'

Andrew made a gesture that he passed that one up.

'Twenty-five million times. And the same goes for the rat, and for the elephant. Their hearts just go slower and faster, that's all.'

'It's a magic number.'

'It's not magic. It's much bigger than magic.'

'And you, the son of an anthropologist!' Wilton chuckled.

'It's the essence.' Timmo went suddenly quiet. 'It blows my mind anyway.'

He threw his arms wide as if to embrace his entire field of vision, the polders with their gleaming fringe of reeds, the silent sepulchral trees, their trunks stippled brown and white on the side turned away from the thin light, the swirls of snow on the fields. Then he broke away and sped on in front of them, flapping his arms and bending his thin legs. He whirled and came swooping back to them.

Professor Wilton was muttering, 'Divine proportion! It "blew the mind" of Archimedes, and it "blew the mind" of Galileo too. It didn't "blow" Einstein's. Not altogether. Just relatively.'

'Oooh,' groaned Timmo. 'What wit!'

He continued at the Professor's side, with a broad and happy grin on his bony face. Ahead, he could see the arcature of the approaching bridge, and then his gaze fell on his father, where

70

he skated beside the girl called Katy Ordel, and the furrow reappeared between Timmo's brows.

At that moment, she fell, and Timmo dashed towards her to forestall that rapt protectiveness his father had already shown when she first arrived on the river that day. He saw him lift her in his arms, and then release her. Timmo sped up to hold out his hand and give her support.

9

Michael was holding out his hand to Katy. She took Timmo's instead, and stiffly, the seventeen-year-old allowed her to thread her arm through his and make mock of her fall's seriousness by leaning against him.

'Wow, I'm whacked,' she said. She held his arm with the hand that had given her the proof she wanted. She thought: this is his son, this is blood made of his blood. I could have done the same. She held on to him, the very substance of that virtuality within her.

For, with the crack of her knee on the ice, Katy felt in her belly the dull ache that she had longed for and that she had imagined daily, hourly, minute by minute over the last week, an anxiety that had become a tinnitus in her ears, and constant drumbeat in the brain. But coming suddenly a cropper, the drag in her abdomen became unmistakable, and fallen on the ice, she was able with surreptitious fingers to touch the cloth of her tight trousers between her legs. When she saw on them a faint, rust-coloured streakiness, she was jubilant. And so she smiled and smiled and smiled, into Michael's eyes.

Then, because she longed to tell someone but could not, she slipped her glove on over her slightly incarnadined fingers and held out her hand to Timmo.

'Are you all right?' he said, talking into his chin with shyness at her closeness. 'Can you carry on?'

'Yes, yes,' she said. The feeling of rapture had not quite faded; she felt as light as helium.

Michael, hanging to one side, said, 'That's a good thing. I thought for a moment you were going to be our first casualty.' He was heavy with assumed heartiness.

She looked at him. She felt herself to be queenly. 'Me? Never.' And she smiled again, a smile tinged with superiority.

Michael had been so pleased at her appearing on the ice, she'd seen the way he fidgeted on his feet as she arrived, and how his face relaxed and his eyes beamed. Katy had come, although she liked to spend the mornings when she had no classes lying in bed, watching the blue cones of gas climb up the calcified ridges of the gas fire and turn them very gradually from bone white dryness to glowing honeycomb; curled over one book, then another, and yet another from the pile she kept scattered on the floor by the bed. They represented other lives, and each one of them seemed a new possibility; she pondered the destinies of heroines like the prospectuses of career advisory centres: Aurora Leigh, high-minded, princely; Lesbia, tormenting Catullus with infidelities; Jean Rhys's hapless waifs, drinking alone in bedsitting rooms; Alexandra Kollontai, a pure flame of loyalty to the revolution. She could be each and every one of these for a time as she read, and still leave time to choose her role in reality too. For her self, like the face that she could alter as she pleased, was inchoate as albumen, and it would, it could, hold the brightness and the colour of any pigment she chose. The consideration of her powerful formlessness sometimes confused her: she chafed to know the limits of her possible incarnations. But more often it filled her with elation.

In this mood, she had faced the lateness of her period with happy heroics. Her daring would be Promethean. Like Aurora Leigh, she would scoff at convention, she would face down her tutors, prove Miss Sidmouth's head-shaking apprehensions false, raise the baby in her room and sail through finals, distinguishing herself. She would be Viva'd, wearing the baby in a sling against her breast. Her friends in college would become a noble and selfless sisterhood: there would be baby food beside the coffee jar in the pantry with the *Song of Songs* poster on the wall. 'I have a little sister, she has no breasts . . .' At least Buttered

Carrots and Semolina wouldn't walk; no perhaps they would. Katy herself ate jars of baby food – they were quick and nourishing. If she moved her desk up to the corner of the bookcase, the cot would fit next to her bed, just. She made mental calculations: the baby would be born in September, so it'd still be under a year old when she graduated. She'd breast-feed in lectures; she'd be told not to; she'd defy them and become a cause célèbre. She might even go to more lectures than she did now, with the baby as a trophy of her new self-definition. She would call it . . . Ishmael, outcast.

Then Katy laughed bitterly and tried to focus on the pages in front of her on her desk. Fear swelled up in her like indigestion. The authorities would send her down. Her principal, in that room with flower vases filled with the college garden's offerings, would wound her to the quick with still, soft disappointment. 'We had our hopes of you, Miss Ordel. Miss Sidmouth tells me you are a girl of some promise. We are all most distressed. You've allowed yourself to be dragged down, just when the world is offering so much to you.' Her thin hand with the scribe's knob on her middle finger would take in the college and beyond the college, the university, in one majestic sweep.

Katy gibbered at her desk. No, no, she begged, listening to the faintest murmuring motion of her abdomen. She considered Michael and she groaned. He was so old, he'd never help her right. He wouldn't have a clue. She thought of the jabbing motions he made with his head as he talked and the way he held a pause, lips parted in a kind of emphatic and laughterless smile, his eyes merry above the frame of his glasses, just before he made the central point of a story or an argument. He was hateful, so decisive in speech, so useless in action. Katy blamed him with the full force of her being, her shoulders and spine hunched in accusation of him. She hardly spared a thought for the man she had really slept with; in her mind it was Michael's child, Michael was incandescent in her imagination. If he had shown less reserve towards her, she wouldn't have looked for reassurance elsewhere that her body, that simulacrum of her self, was powerful enough to draw a man inside her. Tony was just a friend, she'd think about him properly some other time; she went to bed with him so absently, in the midst of the disconcert that Michael had produced when he refrained from taking possession. Tony had served to show her that she was not rejected; yet the puzzle Michael had set continued to fox her afterwards. Not long ago, one afternoon she had gone on an impulse straight to Tony from Michael, and said, 'Am I fanciable?'

Tony shifted, and, adjusting his glasses, replied in the manner of a tutorial, 'Is that a general proposition, or are you asking me if I fancy you?'

'I don't know,' said Katy, and laughed.

He sat down on the edge of the armchair near her, then jumped up again to fetch sugar. It was black molasses sugar, and Katy scooped two large spoonfuls into her mug with pleasure. 'I suppose I meant it generally. But would you sleep with me? If . . .'

'Would I fuck you?'

Katy dropped her eyes and stirred her mug briskly. 'Yes, I suppose that's what I mean,' she said. 'If it were on the cards . . .'

'Shall we try it?'

Tony put his mug down on the hearthstone by the fire. Katy did not correct his misapprehension; she was curious to see, after her long, unconsummated afternoons with Michael, if sex could be as quick, as uncomplicated, as switching on an automatic kettle and knowing that, in a given time, it will come to the boil. The image was vulgar and she had relished it.

When the pulling ache became unmistakable, Katy's first exuberant relief began to fade, and was replaced by a kind of nostalgia for that person she might have been, whose independence would have been a living reproach to Michael, and so a continuing claim on him. At once ardent and withdrawn, he baffled her: with a child, she could have put him to the test, and when he failed, the necessary distance between them would have been staked out for good.

'I'm fine,' she said to Timmo. 'Thanks.'

Timmo spread his hands. 'Any time,' he replied flatly, and left her with a sudden sprint. He moved unsteadily, with long, dashing swoops, towards the approaching barrier of the fens' irrigation works. He was bent forward, his arms and hands swinging across his torso low, like a racer's. But he failed to gather any real speed, for all his effort, and looked as if he were scrambling.

Katy was alone, though the group was all around her, and she felt exhausted. The sun's strength was now at its zenith, but still gleaming palely on the snow crust, catching a sparkle of crystal here and there. She sighed, and looked over at Michael, who was still cheerful as he skated between two other students. How much himself he seemed to be, how custom-made for his own skin and his own mannerisms; how ill-fitting she felt herself by contrast.

He was so confident, even when he didn't get his way, like that day in London when they were together, and he had been at a meeting of the board of a museum whom he advised on their ethnographical collection. It was the first day they had had entirely to themselves, and early autumn, so it was still light when they came out of a cinema after the first evening show. Michael's hand was on the pointed bone of her narrow hips under the wadded coat she was wearing, and she had snuggled into him, suddenly wanting his solidity. He was looking at her, hungrily, there in the rush-hour scurry of Leicester Square. But she was looking past him, unable to respond to his openness with her eyes. His naked admiration embarrassed her. So he did not see what she saw.

'Michael!' she cried out.

They were passing a tramp. He sat on the stoop of a disused building; there were many such in the Square. There were stains on the boarded alcove of the entrance. The Saturday-nighters had been pissing high, leaning back to let the beer gush out of them. The tramp's eyes were drifting, he was laughing with a round mouth like the hole of a tap, and his foot, bandaged in pieces of old socks, tapped the cap that lay open on the pavement. With a waving, unfocussed hand, he was trying to fix a harmonica to the slobbery orifice his lips formed as he laughed.

'Michael!' she cried again. She tugged at him to notice. 'They're taking it,' she pointed.

Three kids of school age were leaning into one another; the two boys gasped with laughter, the girl was lean and unruffled. She had change in her hand. She counted it, and then turned to the beggar. 'Ta,' she said. 'Ta ever so, grandad.' Her voice was full of scorn.

Her two companions echoed her. 'Ta, ta, Grandad.' Their mouths, in their pink, beardless faces, twisted into hangman smiles. Jaunty, on the soft pads of their thick shoes, they began to swing away down the pavement, walking on the balls of their feet, bodies touching one another in the glee of their take.

Katy looked again at the tramp. He was shaking his hand in the youths' direction. It was too lax to shape into a fist, and his face was filled with imbecile good humour.

In front of him the cap was empty, except for a few coppers. Katy was pulling at Michael; she wanted him to act. She felt him beside her, so tall and so ... manly and she was possessed with fury that he could not change what had happened, stop the film, roll it back and play it again, differently. She shrieked at him, 'Do something, do something about it.'

'Katy,' Michael was remonstrating, lazily and with good humour.

She was furious to see him so composed. 'Go on,' she said, and pushed him.

77

Michael jostled through the dawdling crowd. She followed him. The group was ahead, on the corner, waiting for a pause in the traffic flow. Katy saw Michael's look suddenly harden. She became excited. Michael came up behind, and tapped on the shoulder the girl who had palmed the money. She jumped around, with the jerky reflex of someone for whom a touch means hostility. Her face, under a short coxcomb of mouse-coloured hair, was narrow and petulant.

'Did you steal that old man's money?' Michael asked. He sounded uncomfortably cultured.

'Who the hell are you?' One of the boys whipped round. He pronounced the words thickly, as if his tongue and lips were bruised like a prize fighter's.

'You should give it back.'

'Fuck off.' The other boy leaned in, wearing the same mirthless leer he had assumed over his friend's haul. His shoulders rose as he squared up to Michael. Michael, challenged by the boy, was hesitating. Katy looked away. She heard him say, 'If you had some money, would you want me to take it?'

'Leave off.'

Michael brought his hands up in a gesture of abolition, and waved these words away. 'You can't live by force,' he said, with an infinite weariness. But as he moved, one of the boys caught his wrists. 'Pack it in,' he said.

The girl looked at Michael squarely, narrowing the gap between them. Very slowly, ponderously, she swirled saliva around her mouth, as if rolling it into a ball in her blown cheeks. Then she spat a gob, deliberately. It missed Michael's feet.

Katy gasped. The boy's eyes flicked towards her. 'You cunt.'

'You should have more compassion,' Michael tried, uncertainly. His arms were still pinned.

'Yuk,' said one. 'Stupid wanker.' Michael's arms were released, as if thrown.

'Com'n, let's beat it,' said the first boy, jerking his head.

'Fuck you,' said the second, giving Michael the finger, as the three youths, dodging into the choked traffic, sprang away.

Michael heaved a sigh, and then shuddered.

Katy was hot and very scared.

'Do you know I could not look them in the eye?' Michael said. He pulled her almost roughly to his side again. 'I wanted to, but my eyes just slid away. I looked at their cheeks, their necks, their collars, their earlobes, anything, but not their eyes. I was scared. I wanted to stare them down, as we used to do at school. And I couldn't. I stood there, and all that kept on going through my head was "No man is an island" . . . Absurd!'

'They certainly wouldn't have understood that. Anyway, you tried.'

'Can anything be done, does trying reach them? I thought one of them looked just a touch sheepish. Maybe something stirred there.'

Katy shook her head and held tightly to him. 'I can't bear the world,' she said. 'It's such a terrible place.'

'Little one,' replied Michael, 'that was . . . nothing. Really.'

She didn't want him to take an inconsequential tone; she was disappointed that he hadn't made the boys give back the money. 'Shouldn't we go back and give him something?' she asked.

'No,' said Michael.

'Why not?'

'What good would it do? He'd just spend it on drink.'

The absence of a clear moral solution filled her with anguish; she longed to go back to the simplicity of her childhood, when she never would have questioned any dispensation of justice her father made, when nothing he did inspired doubt. Katy longed to find belief.

10

When Timmo began going to school all day, Viola applied to the university to do a postgraduate degree in Aesthetics, and chose as the subject of her dissertation Gerard David's diptych in Bruges, *The Judgment of Cambyses*.

At first glance, the painting seemed a traditionally gory, typically Flemish martyrdom. In the left-hand panel, the victim was lashed down, his face convulsed in agony, while an executioner sliced into the man's flesh with a knife, as if cutting out shoe leather to a pattern, and an assistant, knife between his teeth, parted the skin from the flesh the length of the man's raw and bloody leg. A group of richly dressed burghers and burgesses were standing to one side, contemplating the butchery with such serenity they seemed almost to float. In the right-hand panel, a man was seated on a throne, and the composure of the onlookers beside him appeared even more complaisant and assured, while the glowing colours of the damasks and fine woollens of their heavy coifs and voluminous robes accentuated the impression of confident splendour and unqualified indifference. The enthroned man in fact looked just like the usual pagan emperor torturing the usual stalwart Christian.

In her thesis, Viola unfolded the steps she took towards understanding the story the painting told, and she hoped that as she argued, she revealed the different uses of violence in art. The act of horror, so coolly represented by the painter's immaculate verisimilitude, was shocking: pity for the victim's poor flayed mortality surged instantly, and the indifference of the bystanders, so marked it actually seemed a kind of gloating, turned this pity into fierce indignation. In their grandeur and their sterility, they seemed monsters, and looking at them, she pointed out, the viewer identifies strongly with the victim under their gaze, and challenges them across the dividing years to give proof of some humanity and relent. 'But the knowledge that the painted figures cannot melt,' she wrote, 'cannot be redeemed, gives the painting added power: the suspension of time in art cuts off the wicked from the salvation of tears. They are Other, and will always remain so; we, the painting's spectators, divorce ourselves from them, spectators at the martyrdom.'

When Viola, after first being struck by the painting, looked up the story of Cambyses, the painting's meaning was instantly inverted. That was why she decided to use it in her thesis as a prime example of the dependence of aesthetic value on meaning. For Cambyses turned out to be the executioner's victim, not the seated potentate, the 'judgment' was being given against him, not by him. The ambiguity of the genitive had misled her: Cambyses was a Persian tyrant, remembered through Herodotus' *Histories* for the arbitrary cruelties of his rule. His subjects rebelled, and when his case came to judgment, it was decided that he should be flayed alive. As an added touch of bizarre, and in Herodotus' eyes, very Oriental refinement, the judges also ruled that his skin be used to cover the seat of the king's throne, so that his successors should never forget the fate of tyrants when they sat in the same place. With this grim warning so close at hand, they might remember to act with justice and mercy.

When Viola read this anecdote, she realised that it changed the alignments, both between the figures in the painting, and between the painting and the visitors in the museum. Suddenly the 'martyr' was a monster; his sufferings a just, if severe punishment for the crimes he committed when he was a great sovereign. His gritted teeth and staring eyes no longer expressed the bravery of the innocent when tortured, but the contumaciousness of the wicked when they meet their deserts. Suddenly, she pointed out, the haughty bystanders are ourselves, seeing that justice is done to a man who has abused his responsibilities. We are suddenly united against the victim of the flayer's knife. Or at least Gerard David the painter is asking us to be.

But the delicate and scrupulous attention with which David created the mask of agony on the man's face makes allegiance with those solid and complacent burghers very unsteady. Their victim's pain pleaded for sympathy, but only because it was pain, accurately rendered. The painter's brush strokes conveyed no greater commitment to the victim or to his judges; the same finely blended, patient, careful handling of each of the characters failed to transmit whether scorn or pity is required. The viewer could choose to be on the judges' side, the side of the just, only when the story was explained.

Viola wondered if David had intended to render the loyalties of the painting's internal structure ambiguous; did he perhaps want his audience to see that human suffering is equal, whether the sufferer be good or bad? Did he mean to convey the terrible paradox that Christian martyrdom could look like justice to someone of a different faith? Did he look into the future and see that a sacred subject could be inverted in meaning when the key to the imagery was lost; that the Crucifixion could look like nothing but the grisly execution of a common criminal? Or that St Agatha, with her severed breasts like buns on a dish, or St Erasmus, as his entrails were wound out on a windlass, or St Lawrence slowly roasting on his griddle, might seem to be suffering the barbarous penalties of a barbarous age, but for no doubt barbarous crimes committed?

It was an anachronistic hypothesis, of course. David wouldn't have been able to distance himself, like a modern, from the prevailing imagery of his times and its universally accepted meaning. But it amused Viola to turn positive to negative in the same way as Cambyses' identity and story had done to the painting of which he was the protagonist. As she went on researching, she uncovered something else; the features of the flayed man were the features of a Bruges judge recently found guilty of corruption, and the men who assisted so loftily at the summary torture of his body were members of the Town Council, David's contemporaries, and their wives. It was they who had commissioned the painting, and in their portraits, they showed their satisfaction with a punishment meted out symbolically, through the medium of paint. Their cruelty was no longer taking place in an actual plane; it was a fantasy and an effective one. How that judge must have shuddered, Viola thought, when he saw himself mangled to death under their impassive stares.

The viewer now, she argued, even if he or she knew the story the painting tells, might find that the penalty depicted were too harsh, and the tranquillity of the seamless brushwork too unclouded to convey the avenging fury of the Bruges burghers who unearthed Cambyses' death from the classics in order to hold out a warning to a bad judge. 'Under modern eyes, *The Judgment of Cambyses* rises from its original, almost vulgar level of cautionary tale and becomes a fully articulated tragedy,' she wrote. 'The figures in the painting stir pity and fear at the human condition, at human presumption and human cruelty, regardless of the quarrels and vengeances that motivated the Town Council and were faithfully represented by David. With the lapse of time the violence in the painting has become grander in its implications, because it has been freed from the circumstantial grievances that inspired it, both in contemporary Bruges and in the Persia of the original source story.'

Viola had enjoyed herself hugely. Teasing out the strands of meaning hadn't been difficult, more of a game. But the idea of elucidating pictures until their ultimate meaning might be grasped had since become a passion, and she was now at grips with a far larger problem, a cycle of frescoes that had recently been discovered in the Vatican.

Five years ago, an American historian of Renaissance

architecture, following up some sixteenth-century ground plans of the Vatican buildings, discerned a chamber located in a space under the landing of a private staircase between two large reception rooms in the Borgia apartments. The sixteenth-century mapmaker had inscribed the space 'Bagno di Cardinale Birbarotti' – the bathroom of Cardinal Birbarotti. As the toilet facilities of the papal apartments had always been rudimentary, the inscription roused the historian's curiosity.

Birbarotti was a humanist scholar of Greek, who was appointed by Pope Alexander VI as legate to the last remnant of Byzantium in one of the many attempts to patch up the quarrel between Eastern and Western churches. He spent six years at the reduced court, and the mission proved a failure. But not for the world of letters; Birbarotti had soon found a more pleasant way of spending his time in the Eastern empire than discussing such matters as the nature of the Real Presence in the sacrament. He began reading the Greek manuscripts in the Emperor's fabulous library; he requested that scribes be sent from Sicily, from the Puglie, and other parts of former Magna Graecia to copy and, in some cases, to translate. The Vatican subsidised the needed clerks, and when Birbarotti returned to Rome, he brought with him, in three sailing ships, a cargo of some of the most pagan writings of the ancient civilised world. It included the mystery rites of the temple of Demeter at Eleusis, which have never been traced again since, either in Rome or in their country of origin.

Some manuscripts remained and still remain in the Vatican library; others went astray, into the hands of private collectors in Florence and Urbino and other humanist centres, whose patrons and connoisseurs were in confidential touch with Birbarotti and able to assure him that they would keep safe in the privacy of their libraries the treasure he had wrested from the anathema and bonfires of less liberal churchmen.

Birbarotti's cargo has remained one of the most fascinating, diverse and rich deposits of ancient learning in Western Europe in the fifteenth century, and new discoveries in provincial libraries continue to increase its importance as a source of the hermetic studies of the humanists.

When the architectural historian, Carole Japhet, saw that Birbarotti had built himself a bathroom, she was not very surprised. That Birbarotti should have learned the graces of Eastern hygiene during his stay in Byzantium was not unexpected. There was a much-quoted, derogatory reference, in a letter from one cardinal to another after Birbarotti's return, to 'that perfumed Oriental leopard' (*quel gattopardo orientale profumato*). The 'leopard' stood rampant on the Birbarotti family coat of arms.

After a tangle of negotiations with the Vatican authorities, Carole Japhet was given permission to take a sounding, by piercing through the chamber near the cavity she had located on the map. A scraping of the inner wall of the chamber was taken and the resulting sample sent for analysis. When the results came back, they showed traces of pigment in the plaster, as for fresco painting. Even the Vatican curators became excited.

It was obviously impossible to cut through Pinturicchio's paintings on the Borgia apartment walls, so a tunnel was begun through the floorboards, and a camera introduced into the chamber on the end of a long flexible pipe like a plumber's snake, which was then rotated to take pictures of the hollow space.

When the photographs were developed, they revealed that the four walls of the windowless room were painted all over; the entrance now hung in the air on the west wall, above the staircase, which, when it had been built to give private access to the papal apartments, had been cut through the vestibule to the bathroom, thus necessitating bricking up the latter. To have kept the bathroom in use, a new door would have had to be built, which would have destroyed part of the bathroom's cycle of frescoes as well as a portion of Pinturicchio's on the other side. Rather than destroy, the seventeenth-century builder of the staircase had preserved, almost to the point of oblivion.

A group of art historians immediately gathered in Rome to see the door opened and the room breached. Viola was with them.

The colours were fresh as spring sunlight after rain, the paint firm and lustrous, the quality of the figures exquisite. When Viola stepped off the ladder into that Renaissance bathroom, her hair stood on end. There was dust in the empty cistern, and dust on the marble table where the ewer and basin had stood; a bowl of violet petals stood on it, left five hundred years before to sweeten the fusty air of the closed room. They were brown now, like a mouse nest. But the past itself was made palpable and bright in that room, like a planet that has never known dust at all. Viola stood there, and the heat on her skin burned and her eyes smarted with gazing at the paintings, new-struck, shiny, utterly entrancing, and she was moved to painful depths. But this first access of wonder soon gave way to pragmatism, as one by one the art historians shook themselves and asked, 'But what are they about?'

The narrative remained impenetrable. No saint's life, no theological schema, no conventional cycle of the Passion or the Redemption or other Christian mystery could turn the key to the frescoes' meaning. Viola had been trying for two years to sift the catalogue of Birbarotti's library to find the story – for the frescoes formed a sequence, with recurring characters – on which the painter had based his novel images.

When she found it, then her relationship as ignorant spectator would be altered, her role would develop another aspect, and like the twofold watchers of *The Judgment of Cambyses*, those inside the painting and those outside it, she would become a participant in the drama the frescoes recounted. Whether she would consent, or refuse to consent to the painting's intent, remained to be seen.

Viola took Jimmy's arm. She was breathless. 'Thank God we're taking it slowly. Otherwise we couldn't talk!'

Jimmy laughed. '*We* couldn't talk?' he twinkled at her. 'I'm dying for that drink Michael promised. Shall we try and catch up a bit?' He looked across the reed-choked river's edge towards the polders, beyond a line of pollarded willows that held their maimed trunks up to the swirling, nacreous cloud. The frozen river had led them out of the town.

One by one as they passed the fourth bridge the skaters were touched by a change in the atmosphere. Where they had been sheltered by buildings and by trees, they were now exposed and in open country. Willows had hung their delicate tracery over the ice, but now a stubble of reeds stuck out of the river's high banks, on the crest of the low dykes that guided its stream, and beyond them, the piebald fields stretched in an even deeper silence. They were in open country, where there would be few bridges, and their whirling, falling, swooping and giggling band seemed to trespass flagrantly against nature's white ceremony of stillness, and to desecrate the slow ritual of her winter pulse.

As one and all were caught up in this act of mischief, a communal feeling swelled that alone in the emptiness together they were running against the grain of the world, and their spirits rose as the wild, exhilarating contravention swept them on.

II

'Well, dear lady,' said Professor Wilton, as Viola drew beside him, leaving Jimmy to rejoin Andrew. 'A perfect day for the ice.'

They did not know each other well. Wilton had objected to the entrance of women students and fellows to the college of which he and Michael were members, and Viola felt uneasy with him. His reasons, as relayed to Viola by Michael, were of such a trivial order they seemed comic: no lavatories fit for ladies in the buildings, the college port's fineness wasted on uneducated palates.

'I hope you're enjoying it,' Viola replied.

'Very much, very much.'

There was an element in Wilton's antagonism of self-drama-tising cussedness. He had cast himself, in this respect alone, as the quixotic custodian of tradition, and he played up to the expectations of the progressive younger men with his hopeless prejudice and trenchant malice, delighting in the raised eyebrows and exasperated tempers that resulted after another piece of mischief. 'He put up a motion today,' Michael reported one night, 'proposing a new regulation: "Fellows wearing high heels or other barbarian footwear damage the college lawns and should remain on the footpaths, like visitors." '

'He has a point,' Viola conceded. 'But it's a game for him, and I don't know why he enjoys it.'

Michael went on, 'The other night, at high table, he turned to Dr Lally, that psychologist from Stanford, and said, "Rome fell when capital passed into the hands of widows and their priests. You are both widow and priest. Rome is falling." It's absurd!'

'What did she say?'

'She was very restrained. She's used to nut-cases, I suppose. She said something to the effect that she wasn't a priest, but she was pleased to know that she could be.'

After a pause, Viola said, 'It's sad, that homosexual dream of a pure, male academy.' She could visualise Wilton's ideal college, the students nude athletes in the Athenian gymnasium, the high table a Parnassus of sages and scholars disputing. 'Then we come along and upset it all. But it's so odd, when you think how advanced he's always been in other ways.'

Michael said, 'I think it acts as a kind of control for him: it expresses all the ideas of his background and upbringing so he's free to rebel against them in other areas.'

But Viola felt a need to vindicate herself as a woman, and hoped to engage him as they glided along side by side and reveal herself to be worthy of her teaching post, and, in her own worth, a true representative of the university's female sector. 'You were talking to Timmo?'

'Most congenial.'

'He's doing A-levels this summer. After that, he doesn't want to come up here. It's natural, I suppose.'

'Where does he have in mind?'

'I think he wants to try for MIT.'

'Not a foolish notion. Not at all.'

A silence fell. The sun, as it rose, increased in brilliance, and now radiated through the lifting mistiness of the clouds in a pale gold disc or harvest luminousness. The crystal filigree on the frozen fields scintillated, as they moved along the river between the reedy banks, its glinting facets providing the only movement in the scenery apart from the turning figures of the skaters themselves. But on the willows that stooped down over the ice, the silver encrustation of every twig was thawing under the sun's stronger beam and their trunks shone wet and black.

Viola felt impatient with the old man's brevity. She wanted him to praise Timmo, to question her about him. When at length he spoke, and asked her about her work, she heard a hint of archness in his voice. She responded tetchily, and as soon regretted it. 'Do you really want to know?' she asked. 'Or is this some gallantry toward the inferior sex?'

He turned his face towards her. Under the flossy hair, it looked, she thought, just like Red Leicester, a mass of red veins in a crumble of pasty cheese. The face of a celibate – soft-edged, slack. His only indulgences have been fine wines and choirboys' knees, she thought, and this has spayed him.

'I remember something about a bathroom?' Wilton refused her tone with polite firmness.

Viola, touched with remorse, recovered her courtesy, and then too late noticed that he had, by turning her mood again, shown his dominance. 'Yes. The bathroom of Cardinal Birbarotti!' She laughed. 'It really was the first one in the Vatican palace. But I'm not studying the waterworks, or the fixtures. I'm preparing an article on the frescoes. Their subject matter is hard to understand.'

'I remember,' said Wilton. 'Pinturicchio, wasn't it?'

'Some people think so. They may be earlier. A disciple of Filippino, perhaps. I'm not an expert on attributions. But I'm working away at it, slowly.' She shook her head. Viola then remembered how she wanted to convey the authoritativeness of her work to Wilton, and she added, as casually as she could, 'I'm giving a paper on my progress so far to the Renaissance Studies Conference in Los Angeles next month. UCLA. They're flying me over.'

'Flushed with money, these Americans.'

They skated along side by side. Viola was silenced by such a dismissal of her achievement. She wanted to leave his grudging company. But she hesitated to be abrupt, thinking that by outdoing him in courtesy, she would score against him more effectively than by answering him in kind.

Wilton, after the silence, spoke rapidly, so that his breath, freezing in the air, wreathed around his florid face like smoke. 'I think the Chinese were right', he said, waving an arm elegantly at the stippled trunks of the weeping willows along the river's edge, 'to number five elements. Today with the world fallen under a spell, wood is elemental, too, don't you think? Like rock, like ice.' He chuckled, and breathed out a puff of steam into the air. 'Wood, the fifth element! Of course.'

'They counted wood as well? I didn't know.' She paused. 'There's a Christian heresy I came across somewhere, that proposes another element too. Not wood, but another prime material, a kind of special slime out of which God made Adam and Eve.' She paused. 'We should call Timmo over. He loves to hear this kind of thing.'

'No, no, your son's entirely given up to reality. Loathes symbolism. Facts, facts. The periodic table of the elements. No illusions for young Timothy. But for us, some still have a certain resonance – gold, silver, mercury, tin. They have meaning beyond themselves. As metaphor. But the associations of samarium? Of caesium? Or zirconium? Or cadmium? The young fight against meaning.'

Viola shook her head, smiling silently.

'It's not funny, dear lady. We make no new metaphors. Think of those men of science in your period. Think of Bruno, of Alberti, of Pico, they did not hesitate to use scientific discoveries to create a symbolic order.'

Wilton patted Viola's arm. She looked at him with sudden pleasure. When he spoke again and fervently, there was a new softness in him too. 'Mrs Lovage,' he said, and Viola frowned good humouredly at the name, 'there was a time, when I was a boy, can't have been more than ten, you know, a whippersnapper. Came out on this same river. It was frozen too. Strange how in one's youth there's always more sunshine and more snow. There were some older boys, building a bonfire on the ice. Fire, ice, wood, you see my drift. I had mittens on, the kind without fingers, and I foraged for their fire along the frozen banks, until my fingers were so numb I couldn't feel them, not even when I bit down hard.'

'A fire *on* the ice?' Viola asked.

She looked at Wilton. His small eyes were moist and red-rimmed. He nodded. 'One of these big boys came up to me, a-slither, on his feet, no skates. I longed for him to talk to me. I was on my own at home so much in those days. But he ... he snatched the bundle of faggots from my hands.' Wilton held his arms out as if making an offering to the air. 'And flung me the word, "Thanks", without even looking at me. I stepped down on to the river and watched them. They got a big blaze going. Started roasting chestnuts. The wrong sort, horse, not sweet. I could have told them, not even fire will stop the bitterness. But I looked up to them, I hoped that they could make the taste change, that they'd be proved right.' Wilton laughed, shortly. 'They gave me one. I was so keen to be accepted as one of them ... I was so proud to be included, I ate it. They watched. And then, of course, they all burst out laughing at me. "Are you a half-wit or something?" they screeched. "Eating that stuff?" '

Viola smiled into the old man's soft, red face. 'How awful.'

'Love,' said Wilton. 'Love and its attendant agonies!' He stopped then announced feelingly,

> '*Odi et amo; quare id faciam fortasse requiris.*
> *Nescio, sed fieri sentio et excrucior.*'

'How odd,' said Viola. 'Michael was talking about Catullus recently. He said his understanding of pain was entirely contemporary.'

'Yes, yes,' replied Wilton. 'That stab in the heart those boys' laughter gave me. I remember it now! Just when I was most trying to do their bidding. To please, to please them.'

'Aah,' said Viola. 'That is when we please the least.' She

faltered. 'I try not to try and please all the time. As a rule. Survival's the thing. But tell me, does wood fall through ice?'

'Ours didn't. In the past, when the Thames froze, villages turned out to roast the communal ox. No deserted fields and pathways. Not like today.'

Wilton gestured at the empty white on white of the fields beyond the river. 'Winter *was* different. There was more robustness, more zest.' He paused. 'The common cold, bane of our lives. Did people suffer from it when the Brueghels were painting all those cheerful snow scenes?'

'They must have done.'

'They frolicked and never caught cold. I know it.' Wilton beat his chest under the doubled over scarf, and tucked it more securely into his narrowly cut topcoat. He dropped his jocular tone. 'Our lungs are weaker than the Brueghels' jolly fat peasants' lungs. It's our sins being visited upon us, our meddling, our hubris.' Wilton looked at Viola intently.

She shook her head. 'I know you feel like Michael, that the balance is being upset by constant experiments, explosions. He's still hopeful that one of the parties will commit itself.'

'To unilateral disarmament? Yes, but it won't be the party that wins. That's the nub of it.' Wilton tucked his chin into his scarf. 'Michael's optimism is completely, wonderfully admirable. His unquenchable energies! Admirable. Stimulating. He's a man of the enlightenment, full of power, full of belief in his power. He's a model for us all.'

Viola smiled with pride at hearing Michael praised. Then she said, 'His intensity scares me. He can get quite manic. But that's because I can never manage his kind of conviction. Or yours. Things seem to me so floating, changing from whatever view you take of them.'

'Yes, Michael is blessed with divine fury. It's a real gift. Don't let it scare you.'

'It's what I fell in love with in the first place.'

'Of course it was. Of course.'

She could not share it, but she could watch it. She had been his best audience, in the hall night after night clapping the extended performance of his life, reserving her judgment and her humour and controlling her irritation when she could, which was most of the time when they were first married, but less often since. Between herself and Michael the pattern had been set at the start, when he asked her to march with him on a demonstration against the further development of a missile site fifteen miles from the university. He had not told her he was one of the march's organisers, and that he would be making a speech at the gates of the air force base, but she knew, from the efficient information network of the small town. Still, she had not been prepared for his intensity when she joined him.

She found him at the wrought-iron railings of the splendid white marble University Rolls Library, and the set and strained quality of his face struck her into watchful admiration.

He was talking to a group of students holding banners; his manner was quiet and patient. There was, in each gesture he made, and every inflection of his voice, a quality that Viola found impressive and strangely rousing: he minded.

When he noticed her, he left the group immediately, and came up to her with a brief smile that in its utterly roguish lightness shattered his former seriousness as if he had been play-acting. But he had not been, as Viola discovered on the march; an antic sense of mischief stood alongside moral earnestness as twin pillars in his character.

It was a mild day in early autumn, the start of the Michaelmas term. The air was almost balmy, with a breeze from the south-west that caught the first falling leaves and whirled them over the quiet residential streets they passed through as they left the town for the countryside and the proposed missile site.

Two hundred odd students were marching, and a group of dons. Not an enthusiastic turn-out, but if they all stayed the course, a pledge of commitment. Wilton was there, every inch a Jeremiah with his white hair and his stately pace: he had always combined a curmudgeonly conservatism in private matters with subversive calls for greater responsibility among men of science. The police walked at intervals beside them; Michael spoke to the callow officer at his flank and expounded. The policeman's struggle to keep up his pretence at deafness goaded Michael to reason with ever more intense eloquence: Viola listened. She was moved by the conviction Michael possessed. His description of British vulnerability to first strike missiles and the ensuing holocaust was impassioned. She could see the burned and disfigured victims, the smashed services of civilisation, the contaminated foodstuffs, the tainted water supply, the cities smashed and levelled to a moraine. But she saw it as Michael's interior landscape, a fiction of his skilful contrivance, and could not make the leap into belief. The policeman with pimples where his plastic strap chafed his sparsely bearded chin was only a pretext for the generous deployment of arguments, statistics, rhetoric, she realised. She herself was Michael's chosen audience, and she was delighted by his attention, and she admired his courage and his conviction. She was not won to the argument, but only to the man.

Behind them, a dark-blue bus with high narrow windows bolted flush with the metal followed them as they marched towards Fenfoxton. It kept crawling behind them, judging its low-geared speed to the marchers' steady pace. Its presence nudged the slower demonstrators forward, and they in turn surged against the forward group of marchers, so that the bus's pressure was felt throughout the crowd, even at the front where the bus could not be seen.

Viola grew warm as she walked, for Michael's step was longer than her own, and the pace was brisker than she would have set herself. She pulled off her sweater and tied it round her hips; she had a shirt of checked cotton on underneath, which pulled slightly across her full breasts, and she was conscious that Michael noticed as she smoothed it down into the waistband of her jeans.

'Do you remember that march to Fenfoxton?' Viola asked Wilton.

'Which one, dear lady, I've made that journey so many times.' He shook his head forlornly. 'To no avail, too. Each time, the site is bigger, the signs saying "Danger" are bigger, and there are more of them. There's a new one now, have you noticed? "Hazchem", it says. Sounds faintly Arabic!'

'I'm thinking of the one I first came on with Michael, when ... '

'Ah yes, when they thought they could scare us into silence. Fools!'

Viola tried to seize the exact feel of her recollections, as something kicked her in the heart. Yes, she thought, it was like a profession of faith. We marchers were like nuns, taking vows, feeling that radiant apprehension. We walked to Fenfoxton that day as novices walk up the aisle in the white dress of belief and trust, taking an unaccountable risk on the future and plighting ourselves to the unknown, saying that yes, we have found out its secret, yes, we are filled with the knowledge of it, yes, we demand to be its master.

From the back came singing, at first unblended and hesitant. Then Michael, his face tense with commitment to the song, had joined in. Viola first felt a bubble of laughter rise in her throat: public singing spelt patriotism, armies, church, support of institutions that she scorned as naïve, or, worse still, dangerous. But the voices, rising off-key and hoarse, with a lag in unison between the marchers at the back and those at the front, touched her beyond the point her intellectual scorn could hold and with a lump in her throat she began singing too, quietly, an octave higher than Michael:

> 'Oh, deep in my heart,
> I do believe
> We shall overcome some day.'

When Michael took her hand and squeezed it, her heart leaped.

'We mustn't give in,' Wilton was saying. 'Ever.'

The American Air Force base that was to become the new missile site was surrounded by a high wire fence that cut across the fertile and dimpled fields in straight lines, without a single concession to the sinuous contours of the landscape. The rich agricultural clay around was striped with the recent harvest: the stubble was scorched in welts and here and there the hedges held up singed twiggy branches where the wind had blown the fire. But these traces of destruction were pastoral compared to the grim perimeter marked out by the rigid steel fence and its jutting frieze of spikes and tangle of barbed wire. Beside her, Michael shuddered. 'That could mean trouble,' he said.

'What?' she asked quickly.

'Those guys there.' Michael jerked his head towards the base's gates.

Viola saw the group of men standing in front of the entrance. They were holding banners too. As she drew closer, Viola picked out their slogans: 'COMMIES GO HOME'and 'PEACENIKS MAKE US SICK'. (This last, with graphics of a soldier vomiting over a hippie.)

With three members of the march, who were to deliver a petition to the head of the base, Michael began walking towards the gates. The pickets were jeering. At a hundred yards from them, the delegation hesitated, then rallied and continued towards the gates. But the other marchers stayed back, as the organisers had told them to do. Michael and his three colleagues began their approach, and were separated from the waiting body of the march. The jeering grew louder. Viola could not distinguish the words. The sound was furious; one or two of the picket members were jumping up and down, waving some heavy, awkward banners, some were shaking their fists.

The landscape in front of her eyes seemed suddenly suspended, as if frozen like today, she remembered. Even the wind that had enveloped them so softly on the way had died. She twisted around, jumping up to see what had happened to the police in the bus that had been following the march. She saw it skirt their group, and drive up to take up a position facing the counter-demonstrators at the gates. The faces of the policemen at the windows were like eels'; they peered out close to the darkened panes. But they did not get out of the bus. The police who had walked beside the marchers formed a half-circle, between the marchers and their delegation, which was very close now to its goal. Michael and his friends looked as if they were moving through deep snow, so slow was their step, and so protracted the gradual shrinking of the gap between the deliverers of the letter and the men confronting them.

Nothing conquers time like fear; Viola stood in its grip as if she were carved out of eternity.

With Michael and the others a mere arm's length from the gates, the crowd behind her roared. One of the picketers lowered his banner and lunged. From the back, the marchers surged forward. There was shouting, screaming, Viola was carried forward by the roll and press and hurled against the police who linked arms and braced themselves against the weight of the charging crowd. She was crushed against the policeman Michael had been indoctrinating, her feet were slipping and she wanted to catch hold of him to prevent herself falling, but it seemed an impossible breach of a taboo to touch him. Until she saw his eyes. There was his chin, spotty where the strap had rubbed, and his thin nose under the brim of the helmet, and the hostile set of his shoulders as he held the line against her and her friends, as he strained and heaved with the other policemen on either side of him. But when she met his eyes, they were more frightened than any eyes she had ever seen, more frightened than a kicked dog's, more frightened than her own, she knew.

So she clutched him, and did not fall.

At that moment the demonstrators cheated the cordon. Further down from Viola, on the march's edge, they began running round by the fields through a gap in the hedge and rushed towards the struggle at the gate, whooping and calling. Released from the pressure behind her, Viola whirled around. The road behind her was emptying of marchers: they were running to the fight.

'No, no,' she screamed. She began running herself, but soon fell down on the grass verge of the lane and covered her head so she should not hear the sound of the fighting.

Never had she heard a sound like it, like this oceanic roar of human voices. She was sitting, on a bright September day with leaves wafted by the breeze, and there, two hundred and fifty yards from her, ordinary people were bellowing with rage as they struggled and beat blows on one another. Two demonstrators ran past her, roaring to each other in elation, but intent on scarpering before the trouble deepened. One man collapsed near Viola, sobbing.

'Did you see Michael, Michael Lovage?'

He shook his head. 'Not after the beginning.'

Viola wanted to blot it all out in sleep. She lay back on the verge. It was damp and warm at once, like a sick-bed.

Michael found her there, her head still buried, her face averted. 'Viola, are you all right?' he asked.

She jumped up, rigid, and opened her eyes wide. 'Are you, are you?'

'No bones broken,' he laughed, but there were red spots on his cheeks and his eyes were dilated and swollen.

'Let's please go,' she said.

'But I've still got the petition,' he said. He wiped his forehead with his hand, as he let her hold him against her. He pulled it out from under his shirt. 'Bastards!'

'But you're all right. That's what matters.' She laughed, a bitter cough of a laugh. 'We'll send it by post.'

'It isn't all that counts,' Michael replied 'Not *personal* survival.'

She held her arms around his tall frame and leant her head against his chest and felt a rush of pity for his idealism and his conviction and his earnestness. It was a protective love she had learned again since then, with Timmo when he in turn began to experience the cruelties of the world. It was a tenderness that comes springing up from the knowledge that the loved one's expectations are awry, that they will be frustrated and unfulfilled. With Michael, so many years ago, his commitment to the larger principle above the personal one had seemed so right. But since then it had sometimes seemed callous.

Viola lifted her hair with her gloved hands for a moment and threw her head back. As in Palau, she grieved, as in Palau. 'The police at least have learned better now,' she said to Wilton. 'And they know that allowing counter-demonstrators out leads to real trouble.'

'Yes,' Wilton nodded in reply. 'They learned that for once they could not divide and rule.'

Viola mourned the way she had then felt on Michael's side. Now they sparred to assert their separateness, and she was harvesting her irony's fruit seeing Michael so enthusiastic when he was with others and not with her. She had seen how fast he moved to pick up the girl who fell. His reactions were quick and warm, always. And I have turned that away. But she had had to turn away from him.

In Palau, how Michael had exulted! Viola shivered at the memory. Hunched by the light of the oil lamp at his table, he had crowed and chuckled as he pounded the typewriter that night. 'Fantastic material! Fantastic. I don't think even Makepeace had such an opportunity. Everything is there. Everything!'

Viola on the bed scrabbled at the sheet with her nails. 'What do you mean?' she hissed.

'Don't you see? Caste divisions; witchcraft as social control; and the power base of the priesthood. It's fantastic.'

'What the hell do you mean?' Viola sat up.

'In thought I was the one who was so intense it scared you. What's this sudden deep concern?'

'I don't know how you can talk about caste divisions and control and all that...all that guff. Don't you see what's happening now, happening to that girl?'

Michael was laughing, without humour. 'You're really being very silly, my sweet. Of course it's terrible. From our point of view, I talk about caste divisions and social control because that's what it's about. That is its *meaning*. She was of higher caste than the boy who was in love with her, and so a match was forbidden. But the usual authorities, her parents, his parents, his own sense of his place didn't work to prevent his feeling, so the priests jumped in. It's a golden opportunity for them to show they can restore order when other things have failed. That they're the ultimate authority.'

'But what's going to happen to her in the end?'

'Oh, she'll be put in a special part of the temple buildings for a time. A kind of purification interval during which he'll cool his heels and she'll learn to stop giving him the eye. Then she'll admit to being a witch. You saw her. Then everything will be normal again, normalised.'

Viola did not speak.

'Viola?' Michael turned round with an exaggerated air that he would now pay attention to her problem, footling as it seemed to him.

'All right, I see,' she answered dully. Then, 'But what if she doesn't confess?'

'She will ... they'll only give her water to drink in the temple.'

'You can't just leave her there. You can't just stand by and watch. You're always saying that yourself, when we're in England. That we've got to get committed and do things.'

'It's different here. They have their way of doing things. We're not missionaries, you know. Besides, you know what I think about missionaries. Worthless, meddlesome dangers to themselves and everyone else.'

'But that's hardly consistent with all your ... ' Viola faltered.

Michael said, turning back to his work: 'In England, we're part of the social fabric; we are the society. Here we're intruders – our duties are different.'

'No no,' Viola implored inwardly. She said aloud, 'There must be an absolute moral law, there must. Or we're brutes.'

Michael said: 'It's horrible, of course. But don't be naïve. Any interference on our part here will do no good to anyone.'

'That girl is dying and you are doing nothing.'

Viola set off on her rented bicycle every day. Sometimes she left Timmo on the beach, helping the salt panners scrape the deposits off the drying tanks with sharpened fragments of coconut shell. Sometimes he cycled behind her, puffing furious protest at the heat. She preferred to wander alone, she burned to go back to the hiding place and find her bundle of food gone.

It remained undisturbed. She changed the softened fruit for fresh firm offerings; added a little smoked pork to a new pouch of rice; tried bean curd. The food was never touched. Only once during her clandestine visits to the coconut grove behind the temple did she see the girl again: she was sitting, legs tucked under her as before, in a printed batik sarong on the platform of her penitential dwelling. But this time, ten days on, she leaned against the wall for support and appeared to slumber. Her hair hung down in dirty coils on her shoulders. Once, with a mechanical echo of former vanities, she lifted a heavy hand to fasten a strand with the turtleshell comb.

Viola longed for her to eat. She stood there looking across the shallow ditch at the girl and tears stood out in her eyes. Eat, she breathed, please, please eat.

Viola and Wilton had reached the sluice. Its heavy gunmetal-grey gates barred the river in front of them. There was a stirring of the river here, it was spilling over a weir that adjoined the sluice gates in midstream. The current was slow-moving under the ice, and tugged at the grimy crust on the edge, carrying small pieces down over the lip of the weir like flotsam.

Viola skated close to the verge and looked down. Under a hull of ice, cracked and dull as frosted glass, a thin dribble was boring a hole in the frozen river below. Where its struggling trickle fell the tiny circle of visible water was' midnight black and oily. Around it, the ice, softened by contact, had lost its pearly purity and was crumbly and clouded. On her left, the sluggish seepage of the current through the sluice hardly made a sound, but even its feeble babble struck a blow against the massy gelid surface of the Floe.

The sound of laughter came from beyond the barrier, where the skaters had again gathered.

Viola glided back to Wilton. 'We'll have to go around, Professor, as Michael said. By the fields.'

They scrambled up the bank. It was only a short hobble across the frozen ground to the other side. But the heavy clay clods lay unevenly, and their skates slowed their progress.

'Are you all right?' she asked Wilton.

'Yes, perfectly, thank you.'

She held out her hand to help him on to the Floe again after her. Michael hailed them. He was waving a bottle of cherry brandy. Around him, the party laughed, as in turn each one took it, tilted it back with appreciative greed, and passed it on, wiping red noses and chapped lips and sighing with an exaggerated show of self-congratulation at their shared endeavour.

Viola took the bottle in her turn. She saw the girl with the whitened face standing, mutely, beside Michael. The girl's thin legs under her short skirt and thick bundle of her sweater moved hesitantly as she set off again downstream. The river here passed through a manmade channel cut straight across the fens to drain them; with the sinkage of the fields, its level had seemed to rise, so that they were skating by the wide flat landscape, along a kind of causeway, between embankments.

Her figure is barely mature, thought Viola, and wondered if her own body at seventeen had been so very different. And besides, she has bad teeth: they're too big when she opens her mouth. Then Viola struck out in turn, shaking out her hair in the pride of her own continuing attractiveness, but as tense as the trees, stiff with cold. She was skimming down river, almost in flight above the fields, towards the Hob Nails, where Michael had arranged transport.

2

The Frescoes in the Bathroom of Cardinal Birbarotti

The East Wall

Waves are breaking on the shore, and a fishing boat, riding one of the crests, planes as the translucent surge of water carries it forward, weightlessly. One fisherman is holding the prow, his back towards us, the muscles in it standing out fanwise from the spine; another man is vaulting over the boat's side. It's clinker-built, giving the easy, floating craft the common look of a work-boat. The man has both hands on the gunwale. One leg is almost transparent against the bellying of the hull. and his foot skims the foam in the boat's path as it runs aground. The third fisher's back is arched, and the sail runs down in armfuls of creamy folds from the released gaff that swings loose and heavy above his head. The cloths twisted around the men's heads are striped, and even at a distance, the work can be seen to be an imported Middle-Eastern weave, of several coloured threads and golden gimp. An intricate knot secures the drapery of their loincloths.

On the sea beyond the men, more boats. Nets are hanging over their sides, their sails are still furled as they wait for the day's catch to be complete. The light on the line where sea meets sky is a single white brush stroke; the peachy banners of the sunset still fly high above the horizon, and where the sky meets the rising of the promontory that encloses the beach on one side, it glows a brilliant cerulean, as if it were composed of crushed lapis lazuli. There are sheep on this promontory, just discernible as flecks on the chalky scree of their pasture.

As the eye travels down the curves and bosses of this cliff, where sage brush and small dark clumps of thyme cling on the loose white stone, it reaches a walled city. A great and noble city – not on account of its size (it consists of a few buildings only).

But these are so graceful, so harmonious, so airy, there can be no doubt at all that its builders and its inhabitants were people accustomed to fineness.

And prepared too to defend their desires and their habits, for they set their city in a commanding position on the bluff, above the shining ox-bows of a river that makes its way to the shore, just to the foreground of the fishermen's beach. A massive rampart of well-dressed grey stone encircles the city, with square machicolated towers at frequent intervals. There are archers on the battlements, in narrow-waisted doublets and elegant hose of different colours. Beyond the most distant stretch of the wall, in the distance over which the guard keeps watch, beyond the sheep pastures, an early evening mist scumbles the peaked, rocky valleys between the receding blue of the hills.

The city is paved with marble, cut into plain flags, without cryptic or decorative design. The fortified walls vanish beyond the borders of our vision, and we are standing, with the austere and magnificent pavement spread out at our feet, within the precincts of the great city's streets. On one side, a circular temple of white columns with gilded Corinthian capitals: its idol, a goddess anadyomene, holds up the braids of her sea-wet hair. The temple with its long shady double colonnade – a good display of command over perspective – leads to a loggia in the background where several men are gathered in discussion. In front of the temple there is an open space with a fountain, a sculptured nymph who pours water from a crater. The silvery stream of her libation meets the still surface of the pool. A group of women are approaching with water pots. They are wearing loose gowns of different, light colours, caught by ribbons into swirls of drapery at their breasts, their waists, and again, below their hips. Beneath the rills and ripples of their hem-lines their small pink feet are bare. Some balance the pots on their heads; some stand by the fountain, and with elaborate and ceremonious gestures, appear to exchange greetings. One holds a baby, well-swaddled but arms squirming, to her breast; its right hand reaches towards her face; there is a faint smile around the corners of her mother's mouth, below her downcast eyes.

Closer to us, in one of the loggia's arcades and framed by the central arch's easy arabesque, an older woman is on her knees. Her head is covered by a dark plum-dyed veil, edged in a darker purple stripe. She pulls it down and across her breast with one hand so that the lines of its folds lie taut against her body, making one single serpentine scroll from her head to her thighs as she throws her head back and raises her other hand in the air, imploring with the full-stretched tension of her suffering form.

The young man whom she beseeches on her knees leaps towards her. His arms are held out to her to raise her, his knee is bent as he is poised, half-falling to his knees himself, half-struggling to lift her. He is wearing a doublet of figured red silk with a rich fur collar, caught into a wide, low-slung belt that sets off the slimness of his hips and the breadth of his chest. Below the flared pleats of the doublet's short skirt, his legs are smoothly suited in red and yellow hose; on his straight brown hair there is a round cap, also trimmed in fur, set at an angle. He has not yet caught her up into his arms, but the dynamic of his spring toward her makes it seem as if he has. He moves in profile to us, and we cannot see the look in his eyes, only the alarm and the pity that parts his lips, that have been just touched with carmine.

The South Wall

We are now standing in front of the colonnade, its arches frame the scene, and its slender columns divide our view, across the piazza, of the handsome rose-pink palace on the other side. A coffered door, a course of rusticated brickwork up to the piano nobile, large tall windows, bristling with defensive, but ornamental ironwork balconies. Over the rim of one such balcony, where a family crest is carved, a pair of curtains, made of some light stuff – muslin, voile, perhaps silk – are blowing and, as they lift, the chamber inside is disclosed. The room is in shadow, it seems cool and secret, yet what lies now before our eyes does not have to be picked out under scrutiny like the leggings of the archers on the parapets or the smooth musculature of the fisherman's back. The perspective of the architecture concentrates all our attention on this interior and its drama.

The couch in the room is itself a small chamber, hung about with embroidered curtains from a heavy baldaquin, and on it a girl holds out her arms. They are white, whiter than the lacy froth of pillows and sheets against which she lies, and so slender they might snap in any movement more strenuous than prayer, exclamation – or embrace. The light dazzles from the open window on the right of the couched girl; her face in the shadows is tiny, and she has a pointed chin. Attention has been lavished on her hair: it is blonde, braided, and stuck with jewels. Some locks escape, unruly, flowing in twirls and spirals like the curling edge of a wave studied by a master's pencil. There is something disquieting about the ardour of her look, the eagerness of her attitude. She even seems awkward, as she lies in her accepting nudity and yet refuses the passive reclining somnolence of a Venus, twisting herself in covetous greeting of her lover – he who, lifting the pale coverlet and the foamy sheet, with a brown head of hair cut straight to his shoulders, is answering the call of her outstretched arms and getting in beside her. The young man's clothes, red and fur-edged, lie on the floor in a heap and his white body is naked too. Both, in their nudity, look like children.

The West Wall

The shadows have shortened in the city's streets; the marble paving is glowing rosy in the day's full light, and its precisely cut squares process in ever-decreasing rhomboids towards the piazza, where the fountain's statue can be glimpsed, in profile. We're in an alley that flanks the side of the palace where the girl held out her arms to her young lover. We can no longer see the first floor windows, nor the other corner of the building. We are very close to its imposing wall, and the pretence at fortification of those huge hewn scantlings gives it an appearance of magnificence and menace. The perpendicular plane of the building's flank occupies almost our entire vista, and rises only one metre, perhaps even less, from us. In this narrow space between where we stand and where the palace rises, an old man is rending his clothes, the young man's hand is rushing to the hilt of his sword, while a group of men and women around them turn away with grimaces of horror and pain. They've been scattered, as if by a sudden blast, by the filthy thing, sharp-clawed, horned,with a barbed black tail, that is issuing from the lips of the old man. Against the roseate abstract shapes of the palace wall, the demon cuts a jagged silhouette, so convulsed, so polluting, that we can almost smell its stench.

The lips of the patriarch who has invoked the demon aren't contorted, but firm and serene; yet his hands are grappling with the crimson folds of the voluminous surcoat he wears over another, blue-grey gown; one sleeve, slashed to reveal the fuschia cloth of his ample shirt, whips across his body as he writhes; as he strikes his chest, the other sleeve floats in a voluptuous swirl of cloth. Its bulk creates another clot of turmoil against the smooth expanse of the palace wall. His feet, in pointed soft velvet slippers cut into petals at the ankle, back and front, are set wide apart to keep his balance as he jerks in imprecation. Yet the dignity of his countenance is not diminished, and cancels the horrible spectacle of the monster issuing from his mouth.

Confronting him, the young man reaches for his sword with a rapid grace of movement in his long slender limbs. The anger on his smooth, regular features is mixed with agony.

In the panel above the door set into this west wall, (the former entrance to the bathroom), the palace's stone wall dissolves and the landscape is released to view as sweetly as a sudden fragrance. The girl with braided hair is there, taking a bath in a pool set in a meadow. She is kneeling on one knee, pouring water over her white shoulders from a scoop. She holds up her hair with one hand, her head on one side. Beside her, two attendants, in wisps of clothing, hold out a small towel. Their bare feet hardly make contact with the ground. It is studded with early summer flowers, with daisies, pimpernel, violets, speedwell, and the trailing vine of the periwinkle.

The North Wall

The first horse is prancing, its front legs stepping high over the grassy knolls of the ground where, under the stones, a few wild flowers cling. The hoof of his raised leg points down with its tip, under the taut fleet arch of its neck and its plumed head, reined in hard by the first rider. Arrayed in gold cuirass and gold-hemmed dress, she's mounted astride, her full skirts drawn across her horse to add to the caparison's elaborate composition of saddlecloth and bridle, her small foot sheathed in a mailed boot, the spur a delicate wheel, snowflake-spoked. The winged dragon rising on the crown of her helmet cuts across the horizon, where the rocky defile in which she and her gang of armed maidens wait meets the subdued sky. She is holding a banner in one hand, the reins in the other. Her followers have the same device – a seahorse – on their banners, and their streaming colours interrupt, in a rhythmic sequence, the declension of crags behind them. Her horse is a tall chestnut, fit for drawing a chariot of war; behind her, stepping close as they wait, her followers' mounts are grays, and more delicately made. At a casual glance, they could be mistaken for unicorns. The horses' heads rise and fall contrapuntally one against the other, and even though they're at a standstill now, we can sense their temper and their speed.

One of the amazons is leading a riderless horse; she's twisting in her saddle to look behind her, in the direction covered by the gaze of her General on the chestnut, at the gate in the city wall that is standing open. From it emerges the slender figure of the youth. He is blindfold, and he seems to stumble. But his fingers are intertwined with the fingers of another warrior, who in gold breastplate and helmet has materialised beside him in a mandorla of fire. She glances back over her shoulder at him with an expression of grave mercy on her face. All of her is gold, as if she had been chased in metal by a goldsmith; the breeze lifts the robe that swirls around her legs beneath her armour, and plays in her long hair. Ethereal, kin to air and fire, she buoys up the heavy, sightless boy, as she bears him away towards the detachment of amazons. Beyond them, on the speckled water of the bay, an ocean-going vessel rides at anchor.

3

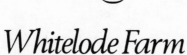

Whitelode Farm

'Like diamonds we are cut by our own dust.'
John Webster, *The Duchess of Malfi*

I

'My ankles hurt,' said Katy, wriggling one foot and then the other in the air as she stood in the lane leading from the channelled river to the Hob Nails.

'Mine too,' said Timmo, hopping about beside her, as he took off his skates.

He nearly toppled, and she put out her hand to catch him. 'Steady!'

'Thanks. Wet socks after all that grief'd be too much.' He got his shoes on, and tied the laces of his skates around his neck. 'Suppose Dad's been lecturing you about how-to-save-the-world?' he said, as they began walking towards the pub's garden gate, where Michael stood, bowing his guests through. Timmo's sharp, dark face was not as filled with malice as his tone. He turned almost appealingly to Katy.

'No,' she said, 'not really. Well a bit. But I like it. I like being told things. I find it easier to make up my own mind when other people are clear.'

'He's a real wanker, I think.'

'Oh!' The cry escaped Katy unwillingly. It seemed naïve, and she hated to appear so. But she was amazed that Timmo could talk so of his father, who seemed to her so authoritative and so knowledgeable.

'Come on, admit it. He's a bore, a big, fat bore.'

She wanted to say, I don't understand you. He's admirable, he's exciting. But, now that her very flesh was no longer in danger from him, she couldn't summon the same conviction as before.

After a pause, she said lamely, 'Why do you think that? Nobody else does.'

'Look, when I was working on a building site one holiday, to get some bread together, he made me take my jeans off before I came into the house. I had to keep clean trousers in the umbrella stand.' Timmo huffed at the memory.

'Why on earth?'

'Said I made a mess, looked a mess.'

'How awful.'

'Petty.'

'Yes, that's mean.' Katy watched Michael, arms extended. He was nodding and laughing as he was joined by the others. The pleasantness of that energy and resoluteness she so enjoyed in him was visible to her, even at a distance.

'Is that really true?'

Timmo dropped his eyes. 'It only happened once, and it had been raining.' He paused. 'The umbrella stand bit was my idea.' Katy's eyes slid sideways, and looked at him, where he sulked.

'So you like fighting him? What did your mother do?' She said the words 'your mother' as lightly as possible, but as she did so she felt a quivering inside, both of liking and of fear, of the woman she had first met on the ice, but whose photograph she knew well from Michael's college desk.

Timmo's eyes met hers, and a gleam of mischief appeared in them. 'My mum's the best in the world, I always tell her so. She's on my side.' He thumped his chest, mock dramatic. 'I'm her boy.'

'I was Daddy's girl, too,' she said, slowly.

'He's snuffed it?'

'Don't,' she said.

Timmo's archness vanished, she noted, instantly at her moment of distress. 'I didn't mean to be ... oh,' he groaned, 'I'm so crude. I never say things right. I'm sorry,' he nodded emphatically.

They looked across the fields towards the pale gleam of the sky on the horizon, where snow and cloud met in curds of mist. A silo stood alone, at a junction of two narrow roads; the snow had slipped off its steel skin and off its spindly and angular legs; against the white sky and white earth, its dark and skeletal form seemed to be inching its way forward with difficulty, like a broken-backed insect, towards a more inhabited and clement resting-place. Timmo shivered, and rubbed his ears in his turned-up collar.

'Don't worry. It was some time ago.'

'Let's make tracks,' Timmo said, dropping his eyes.

'What's that?' asked Katy, pointing to the silo.

'Oh that,' he said. 'Dad hasn't told you about that?'

Katy shook her head, inquiringly. 'It's strange looking,' she said.

'It's a food disposal unit,' Timmo scoffed. 'Used to be a granary – different, of course. When I was ten, I used to walk over to see the sludge pour out of the funnel at the bottom, masses and masses of it, oozing out, like out of a great toothpaste tube. That was when it was full of silage, and a cooperatively owned thing, for the farmers around. They clubbed together for a time to use it. All together. Then they quarrelled about it, what do you expect? Next thing we hear, the government's taken it over. What for? No one knows. Then, suddenly, lots of trucks come one night and fill it up to the brim with food. Corn on the cobs right up to the top, then they set fire to it, right? It's like a huge garden incinerator, and all the stuff no one can sell any more because of the rules about prices and export is brought from round here and put in it regularly and burned. Dad complains, of course. He writes letters, of course. And what d'you get? Nothing, of course. Every now and then, this lovely smell comes wafting over the fields at home, like toasted muffins or roasting peanuts or hot chestnuts, and there it goes, all that lovely nosh, up in smoke. Ha ha, how great, just how great, up in smoke. Who cares, who wants it anyhow? Just a few million people somewhere else, and who gives a fuck for somewhere else?'

Katy thought, 'You sound just like Michael. Except brasher.' She could hardly say this aloud to Timmo. But she smiled to herself.

'Why are you smiling about it?' Timmo beat his hands together. 'What on earth is there to smile about?'

Katy's face straightened fast. 'I wasn't smiling at that. It's appalling. I can see that. I was smiling at ... well, you, your indignation.'

'Yeah,' said Timmo. 'And where does that get us? Nowhere, and fast, like multiplying zero again and again.'

As they entered the steamy pub, Katy pulled off her cap and felt her ears begin to sing with the heat. She was glad to get to a lavatory, and pushed past Timmo with a relieved nod. The Ladies was outside again, in the inn's courtyard, and when she had repaired as best she could the stain of her first flow that day, she stood at the pub outhouse's old china sink to wash her hands. But there was no hot water, and she grimaced at the cold trickle from the tap.

She remembered then the first day of her menarche, when she had been as unready and as unequipped as today, and went in to kiss her father goodnight. She had dropped on to his knees with the routine impulse of long habit, as he was sitting in his low and comfortable armchair. Only as she felt his legs under her thighs did she understand how deep a transformation had been wrought in her flesh, so that she recoiled from her father in dismay as he, also with the dullness of habit, folded his evening paper on to the arm and put both arms around her to receive her kiss upon his cheek.

'Well, my little lady,' he said. She wanted to withdraw from him then on the instant. Terror that she smelled bad took hold of her, horror that he might notice her sudden womanhood flooded her with shame. She jumped away, stood up, keeping her distance. He picked up his paper again, seemed unaffected.

'Not too dull for you, staying here all summer?' he said, distantly, as his eye began to read the sports pages again.

'No, Daddy, no.'

'So much to do in a new house. Your mother and I, we've had our fill of travelling.'

'I know. I don't mind.'

That spring her father had been posted home, for the first time since Katy was born, and the house they had been allocated, a former Victorian rectory near the army base, had not been done up for twenty years.

That same summer, the workmen left and Katy's father decided that the remainder of the budget the army had generously provided for the Ordels' last posting before retirement would be spent on a new lawn.

'A glossy, thick, emerald carpet,' he had said, looking out on the churned mud and mortar the builders had left in the once-tended and sheltering vicarage garden. 'That's what we need. I know it's hackneyed, but England is a green place – in here.' He tapped his forehead between his eyes. 'I want to see it like that – out there.'

The Ordels had lived with tarmac and concrete, desert and dust too long; in the western hills, he would bathe exile's eyes in the green shade that, abroad, was the enveloping light of all his memories of home. 'England is the only place, Kate,' he'd say, 'that viewed from three thousand feet still looks green. Except perhaps Ireland. The rest of the world looks ... scorched. As if Phaeton's chariot had passed too close everywhere else. England has the best climate in the world.' They were looking out on the red-gold flatlands of Aden. 'Sand!' he sighed.

'I thought it always rained in England,' said Katy.

'No,' he answered. 'But it rains enough to keep things green.'

'What's Phaeton's chariot?' she asked.

He put her on his knee and told her.

That September, when they were first installed, he prepared the ground to receive the new lawn. Katy kept him company. Sometimes he allowed her to help him. He gave her an old, cracked bucket the builders had left behind, and she followed him, gleaning the stones he dislodged as he turned over the earth.

'Not too deep for a lawn; mustn't disturb the soil too much,' he said, as he leaned on the spade with his foot against the haft and broke up the harsh clay. His spade sliced it into sods with hewn sides in which the silex left gleaming traces. Now and then he stooped to pick up a stone, and tossed it into a small cairn which Katy then dismantled, patiently transporting bucketfuls to the tip in front of the house that the builders had promised to take away. They did not speak much. The rubbly ground was gradually sifted, and like a pile of threshed corn, began to look smooth-grained and hospitable to growth.

Down her father's back ran a band of dark sweat, and a spattering of grit mingled with the sweat on his brow. Now and then he straightened and, bringing his shirtsleeve across his face, wiped the drops out of his eyes and smeared the grime, like a child in blackface for a pantomime.

> 'When Adam delved and Eve span,
> Who was then the gentleman?'

he called to her. There was a twinkle in his eye.

'Don't overdo it, John,' warned her mother, shouting from the kitchen door. 'You're not used to it, not any more.'

'I'm fit as a fiddle,' he replied, and immediately returned to the challenge of the heavy, inert clay.

Together, Katy and her father trod it in, working from one side of the patch to the other in a shuffle, again and again, while, slightly hoarse, John Ordel hummed old tunes to which he had danced in officers' messes all over the world.

The weather, in their narrow valley, was blowy; the first leaves of the fall drifted over the prepared terrain. Coming from opposite corners, stamping in the crumbled surface of the soil, they were, Katy remembered, staring into the basin in the wintry yard, absolutely happy. Her father's face was so young, all streaked with sweat and mud, the formality of his short hair and small moustache suddenly gave him a kind of wolfish handsomeness, like an old Hollywood star; his lean, tense body, that always seemed clenched, as if to take a blow without crumpling, suddenly seemed designed not for the arts of war, but for play. Katy, her awkward fledgling limbs piped into narrow jeans, executed a soft-shoe shuffle, crossing the ground pigeon-toed and deliberate, and found a delirium of satisfaction in the footprinted track of trodden earth she left behind her.

'You're doing fine,' he called, from his own track.

She called back, gaily, 'It's not exactly difficult.'

Her father always hated it when people wanted to help – speed, competence, effectiveness were his gifts, and he suspected bungling everywhere.

'Can't I rake too?' asked Katy, when they had been over the ground once to firm it.

'*Is* there another rake?' John Ordel's tone was inconsequential, but he didn't manage to hide from Katy his reluctance to have her work.

'You *know* there is,' she protested, with elaborate impatience. She went to the collection of tools leaning up against the house, and took out a light leaf fork.

She knew he'd say it wasn't appropriate. 'But I can do a little with it.' She set to; she could hear her father grunting with the effort he was making to loosen the topmost layer of the soil once again and pulverise it yet more finely to receive the turves' roots. Katy knew his grunts were also signals to her, to show her how he laboured and at the same time how determined he was to race her, to prove how much more he could accomplish, and how much faster, how unnecessary her help was. It made her both affectionate towards him and impatient, but when he came over to the small area she had raked over, and began covering it again, stooping to pick out the tiniest shards and toss them on the cairn, she was not angered by this unspoken criticism, but posed herself on her rake with an exaggerated air of resignation, until he had returned, unsmiling, to the ground where he had been working. This small defeat made her smile, and she resumed her rhythmic scratching of the earth, crumbling it to a level tilth in which the grass would sprout and flourish.

The turf was piled up in the garden in rolls, as if in a carpet shop. John Ordel carried the turves one at a time to the prepared ground, and Katy, on hands and knees, unrolled each one as smoothly as if it had been a runner. The grass knitted together the layer of earth under each turf, and Katy laughed at the knotted pile's startling artificiality. The lawn was pieced together and pressed together until the seams between the rolls of turf showed only as a slight ruck on the surface.

John Ordel worked with dogged untiringness. Katy stood by, brought her father a beer; exclaimed her approval as the pelts of green gained on the exposed flesh of the earth.

When it was done, the evening light slanted across it and heightened for Katy its peculiar theatricality. Laid so expeditiously, the new lawn seemed scenery, ready to be struck after the performance and to disappear as quickly as it had appeared. The weight of the sun seemed to be sucking down the cloudrack with it as it sank; its rays were splintered by the two great elms just beyond the garden's fence.

'It's beautiful, Dad,' said Katy. 'It's just like a stage.' She leapt on to her hands and was upside down. The turf was soft under her fingers, the sun, the trees, the clouds revolved in her sight; her feet flew over her head, and the first, slightly sickening vertigo gave way to exultation. She cartwheeled once, twice, three times, describing an arc around the lawn her father had made.

She heard him cry out: 'Good God, I've been stung!'

She dropped on to her feet again. The garden skidded about, she could not focus, the lawn was a deck, the elms masts and they were heaving to in the blast of a terrible wind. Why was he lying on this rocking deck? Why had his hands flown to his face? That gurgle coming out of his throat, what was it?

She ran towards him; it was hard to keep straight. The lawn was tipping away from her, and her ears were buzzing loud enough to sicken her.

'Daddy, Daddy,' she wailed. She fell down beside him. She feared to touch him. To take his hands away from his face seemed profane. 'Daddy, wake up!' She was screaming into his covered face. He did not move; his limbs seemed to have collapsed upon themselves, and he lay there awkward and angular.

Her mother was running towards them from the house.

Katy cried aloud, 'He's been stung!'

Alice Ordel dropped to her knees; she took her husband's hands away from his face. His eyes were staring open into the gusty sky with its tatters of evening cloud.

'John!' She began slapping him.

'Mum!' Katy seized her mother's wrists. 'Don't touch him!' She was crying.

'Let me alone!' Mother and daughter grappled on the grass.

'Why did you have to hit him? Why?'

'You little fool, stop it.' Her mother fought her way free from Katy's grip. 'Help me.'

Strength ebbed from Katy. Her knees and hands turned to water, and she hovered helplessly as her mother struggled to lift him.

'Help me!' she commanded again.

Katy managed to focus, and transmit the message to her limp limbs, to take up the heavy burden of the big man's inert body.

'We must walk him round.' The new lawn received his stiff, dragging progress on its springy virgin cushioning. They pulled him between them, but his head fell back with those open unseeing eyes, and his feet dangled, turning inwards like a doll.

'It just can't be,' wailed her mother. 'I told him not to!' But they knew they had to let him down again and carry him like that, like a piece of furniture, into the house. When they reached the sofa in the sitting-room they tried to arrange his limbs in a natural position, so that he would look less ungainly and more like himself. Then her mother, looking askance, closed his staring eyes.

It was for Katy as if her heart had been cut out of her; as if she had been lain on an altar, like the white man in a story of human sacrifice among the Aztecs she had read as a child, and her chest stretched tight as the skin on a drum so that the knife of the priest could pass cleanly through it and scoop out her beating heart and throw it on to the sacred flame.

This pain was lodged in Katy like an illness; the completed lawn was the last thing Katherine Ordel had been able to see through to its end.

2

When Katy came back in, Michael was hovering in wait for her. 'You are enjoying yourself?' he said.

'Don't ask me all the time.' She frowned, took a cigarette from her bag, and with stiff fingers tried to light it before Michael struck a match for her. She looked at him; his mouth, with its good-natured and confident curve, compelled her. She felt her lips tremble, she wanted to hold on to him, and put out her hand to his arm.

'Not here,' he said under his breath.

'I don't know why,' she said, 'but I was thinking of my father.'

Michael laughed. 'Oh no,' he said. 'Don't do that. It makes me feel old, and guilty.'

'No, not like that,' she said, quickly, to forestall another assurance of his frustrated desire to look after her. 'He thought he had been stung. But it wasn't a bee. It was a thrombosis, in his leg.'

'Come, you need a drink.' Michael went over to the bar, where his other guests were gathered. She waved refusal at his Bloody Mary, and asked him for a beer.

When he handed her the moist, warm glass, a glitter of proprietary appreciation lit up his eye, and was not missed by Jimmy, who raised an eyebrow at him in mock reproof.

'Darling, I think I'll take the first lot now,' said Viola, coming up behind them. 'Andrew and Jimmy. Timmo, if he wants.' She turned pointedly to Katy. 'Would you like to jump in too?'

Katy could not make her eyes meet the woman's. They slid away from her, refusing to obey her mind's instructions to face her innocently. Under the black-etched lids her gaze dropped uncomfortably to her bleary glass.

'I haven't quite finished this drink,' she mumbled.

'That's all right,' said Viola. Her voice clanged harsh in Katy's ear. 'You come with Michael later. Okay?'

She turned to Michael. He told her, breezily, he'd bring Katy along, and round up all the others. 'Soon, promise.'

'Yes, you must all be famished.' Viola leant towards Michael and took him by the sleeve, pulling him to one side of the group at the bar. She wanted to say, Michael, you must help me. The huge meal she had prepared waited at home for her guests; something about their imminent descent on her filled her with foreboding, for she had worked hard, and she was frightened her efforts would be disregarded. She remarked irritably, 'You're not going to hang round here for ever?' She eyed his drink pointedly. 'There are at least twenty people arriving at the house in . . .' she looked at her watch aggressively, 'only half an hour. One for one-thirty was the time *you* said.'

Michael was mild, he folded Viola's hand on his arm in both his, and leant close to her face. 'You don't have anything to worry about, sweetheart. I'll be there on time. Even if I weren't, you'd cope without me. You always do.'

Viola softened. 'Timmo,' she called, gaily. 'Andrew, Jimmy! First bus for Whitelode leaving now.'

Timmo joined his mother. He'd been having a beer in the corner, talking to the barman with an obvious display of boredom in his parents' friends' company. His head poked forward as he walked, with a hangdog insolence that Katy noticed with approval. He looked effectively cut off from his surroundings, marooned in his youth, and she felt a kinship. The exchange between Michael and Viola had shocked her; she hadn't bargained for their irritable intimacy. It was clammy in the pub, and the fug of beer fumes and thawing woollen clothes was stifling; with the nagging pain in her stomach, the cherry brandy, the beer, the effort on the ice, Katy's field of vision was shrinking. Michael, slipping Viola's gloved hand between his and leaning so close to her face, loomed up in front of Katy's eyes misshapen, his winning look and gesture of conciliation distorted as in a fish-eye mirror.

As she held tight on to her glass, she avoided Michael's attentiveness, which had returned to her at Viola's departure.

'Little one,' he was whispering. 'Not good?'

Katy fought back an infuriating desire to cry. 'Just great,' she said bitterly.

'My darling,' he said, and, flinging away his awareness of the remaining guests in the pub, he bent Katy's head to his chest and stroked her hair. Then, conscious of his risk, he pushed her away.

Behind him, Michael heard his son's voice. Timmo was at the bar. Michael turned about quickly.

His son looked across at him, and at Katy. Or did he? He said, 'Mum thought some people might want orange juice, and there isn't much at home. She sent me back for some.'

'Good,' said Michael absently. 'We're on our way.'

He left Katy and went over to Wilton, who was drinking with two of Michael's students, and suggested they leave for lunch. He was wondering, as he watched Timmo's carefully sauntering figure, how much his son had seen of Katy's tears, of his placatory caress.

The others were keen to leave, and drank up quickly. Michael called out to Katy. She joined them, huddling herself against the tooth of the cold once they'd passed out of the muggy saloon into the frosty country outside again. He opened the car door but she hung back, aloof, for the others, and climbed in the back with the students. Her white face looked pinched.

My wounded sparrow, he thought, with tenderness, as he reversed out of the parking space where he'd left his car that morning. It moved him deeply that he had the power to hurt her.

'Dammit,' said Viola to Jimmy, who was already sitting in the passenger seat of her car, waiting for Timmo.

'What's the problem?' asked Jimmy.

'Michael's got something for that girl, I know it. Damnation.' Viola spat out the words bitterly, grinding at the gearstick to find reverse.

'Darling!' said Jimmy. 'You're not jealous? Of that sickly looking little thing?'

'That's just it.' Viola paused. 'Sickliness. Michael loves that. It makes him feel responsible, big and strong. Ugh.' She fell silent as Timmo came back and pushed the cartons of juice on to the back ledge behind Andrew. 'Thank you, darling,' she said to her son.

She backed abruptly into the road. 'The roads are very icy, Viola,' said Jimmy warningly.

'I know,' she snapped. 'I'm not going to drive at sixty miles an hour, you know.'

'We know you're not. You're brilliantly competent at the wheel, as in all things.'

'Thank you, dear,' said Viola. 'You're a tonic.' But this, she thought, this is beyond my competence. She caught sight of Timmo's profile, looking out of the window from the back seat, and a memory stirred, of another profile and another gaze whose meaning she could not read.

'I'm enjoying myself,' Jimmy went on. 'Though I have to add that I've given my ankle a horrible jolt out there, and will need a lot of care and attention from you, Andrew, and you, Viola darling, when we arrive.'

'Badly, really?'

'Yes, it's throbbing.'

'All right,' said Viola. 'I'll look at it.' She sighed, and turned through a ramshackle gate at the entrace to her home. The car bumped on the rutted surface of the driveway.

Whitelode Farm, Hartbridge, stood near the river, by a brook – the Whitelode – that ran from the Floe along the line of the fence in front of the house, bent around in view of the kitchen, and disappeared at the bottom of the garden in a slushy mere where Michael had planted dark-leaved, overshadowing gunnera. It was a Victorian farm, with double gables over broad, candid windows; the white paint on the frames looked chipped and grey against the brilliancy of frost, though in summer the comfortable, scuffed house looked almost glossy and pristine against the neighbouring fields' deep and dusty stretches of wheat and dazzling sweeps of golden rape. Only Timmo in his hunger saw his home's time-worn look as exhaustion and not experience; Michael and Viola's friends loved the interior's even-tempered charm, and its odd situation, on the brink of water rushing to return to earth and darkness.

Viola drew up with a sharp tearing on thin gravel past the front lawn, and stampingly led her party through the porch, a dainty Gothic affair with a pointed finial and stained-glass windowpanes. She told them to throw their scarves and hats and mackintoshes on the bed in Michael's ground-floor study.

'Make me a poultice, darling, do,' wheedled Jimmy. 'Of local clay, heated up to boiling point. Like my old nan used to do.' They were crossing the stone-flagged hall into the clutter of crockery and postcards in the old unmodernised kitchen.

'I don't want to be your old nanny. I want to be a carefree young thing. I don't want anyone depending on me, I don't want anyone asking anything of me. Instead ...' she waved at the broad kitchen table, where she had arranged salads she had chopped and dressed with attention to the rich, contrasting colours of the herbs and vegetables, a huge cheeseboard, piles of chola bread and long French loaves, and a fluted mould of chicken in aspic, with spears of tarragon under its golden translucent surface. 'I do all this, and Michael's getting drunk in the pub.'

'I know,' said Jimmy. 'Men are beasts.'

Viola laughed. 'I'll have a look at that ankle. Come up to the bathroom.'

She shook out her hair, and smiled at Andrew. 'Find Timmo, wherever he's gone. And get him to help you build up the fire.'

As they went up the shallow treads of the stairs, the coir matting knubbly underfoot, Viola said, 'But it bothers me, all the same.'

'What?'

'Michael frisking about with that girl.'

'I know, darling,' said Jimmy, and gave a slight giggle. 'You heterosexuals, so monogamous. You expect too much. Too much loyalty, too much intensity. You take it all to heart too much. Andrew'll be gone sooner or later. Will I carry-on? Oh no.'

Viola's breath caught in her throat. 'What are you saying?' she almost shrieked. 'You mean something is going on?'

'A passing fling.' Jimmy's jocularity faded.

Oh no, she was wailing inside. She opened the bathroom cupboard. Yes, the elastic bandage was still in the medicine chest. She found it distractedly. It was a relic of Timmo's school-days and its red and black packet, with a poor sketch of a nurse and a limp wrist, recalled for her sharply the commotion she experienced each time her son came to her jarred and shaken from some game when even the post of goalkeeper on a good side had not saved him from falls and punches.

Jimmy sat on the low wicker chair in the chilly bathroom and, chafing the sore joint, held out his pale foot. Viola unrolled the wad of bandage, and snipped it through slowly, with blunted scissors. It was comforting to repeat these actions, so long abandoned. But the comfort did not blot out her pain.

'But she's young enough to be his daughter ...' she faltered. 'And you know about it! Why didn't you say something?'

'I thought you knew, I suppose.'

Viola handed him the section of elastic, pulling it wide. 'Here, just slip this on. It'll hold the ankle firm.' Sickeningly, she saw plainly how her own assumption of maternity in her attitude to all the world had defined her and diminished her, restricting above all her generosity to Michael and her fulfilment of his needs.

'Mm,' said Jimmy, with appreciation. 'That feels much better.'

She sat on the edge of the bath beside him, and pushed her hair back with her hand with unnecessary roughness. 'It scares me. Oh God, how it scares me. When Michael gets hold of a feeling, he can't let go. It's not like you at all.' She looked at her friend with panic in her eyes. 'He won't see things from another point of view. When it comes to politics, his ... intransigence ... is well, noble, but when it comes to people, he's reckless.'

'Viola!' Jimmy stood up and tucked his chin into his neck as if reproving a child. 'What's happened? Come now. Michael's just making a bit of a fool of himself with a skinny, pasty little thing. Don't you worry about her, not for a second. She'd really be a bit more suitable for Timmo.'

Jimmy paused, and his eyes met Viola's with sudden collusion. He gave a short, coy laugh. 'My dear! Really!'

He put his weight full on his ankle and sighed with relief. 'That really has given it some support. Thanks.' He patted her arm. 'Michael is just going through a phase of loving himself, intensely. It happens. I know about narcissism, believe me. We gays do. He looks at her and thinks he's admiring her, but what he's admiring is his own big cock.'

Viola flinched.

'Yes, yes, and I know he's got a big cock and I know you don't mind my being crude. Don't pretend you do. You love it.'

Viola made a choking sound in her throat.

'At least you can still laugh. He's looking at that pale little thing and he's thinking, I'm this terrific omnipotent male and she's in my power. But is she? Isn't that rather a sad delusion on his part? She's probably just a bit flattered by his attention, like most students are when a teacher seems interested in them. They're starved of that most of the time. You should be sorry for him, Viola. I mean it.'

As they came down the stairs again, Jimmy gave Viola an encouraging nod as she began to greet the jostling, crowing guests unwinding themselves from their heavy clothes in the hall.

Michael had arrived, and was dashing from one knot of guests to another with a foaming jug of egg-nog in one hand, and wine in the other, which he poured with abandon into the eagerly offered glasses.

'What's in this amazing brew?' asked one.

'Grand Marnier, brandy, whipped eggs, I don't know what else. Ask Viola,' said Michael, grinning with mischievous pleasure and passing on. 'There's wine too, lots of it, when you've warmed up enough inside.' Now and then he rumpled his hair with one hand, almost shy at the sudden coming of all these people to his home.

Viola was laughing now, tying on a small apron over her well-ironed cream silk blouse and wide navy-blue trousers in order to identify her proper role: she liked to feed people.

When Michael came round the kitchen table to help her hand out glasses of egg-nog, he watched her crumple up the last film of cling wrap from one of the salads and said, 'You shouldn't have taken so much trouble. They'd have been happy with bread and cheese.'

But taking trouble gave her pleasure. She smiled at him under the fringe that fell forwards and adjusted once more the slide in her hair. 'I like it,' she said weakly. 'As you know.' When she would rather Michael joined in the ready and accepting praise of their friends, he always tried to prevent her cooking.

'Where's Timmo?' he said.

'Somewhere,' said Viola.

'Couldn't he make himself useful, just for once?' Michael was irritable.

'He'll help with the clearing up, you know he will. Besides, he always picks if it's around, and it annoys me. He never eats properly.' She wanted to control the way her food was eaten; feeding people was not enough.

'We've something in common after all,' said Michael, poking out a juicy lump of chicken breast from the centre of the jelly and giving her a challenging wink. 'And I'll be off, before you start screaming at *me*.'

How boyish he still was, she thought with a kind of craving, as he turned through the door on a light step and vanished across the hall to the living-room where the fire was lit and the party was drinking. His body was still lean, though perhaps a little scrawny with age, but at least scrawniness was better than the slack podge afflicting so many of their contemporaries. His hair was brown, and though it had thinned, it was still curly and often wild. Timmo had inherited her hair, dark, with a weak wave; she had often wondered how deeply it would have changed his shrewd sharp-featured face if it had been topped by his father's disarming mess of curls. She smiled to herself as she swept some last kelp-like parings of cucumber peel off the chopping board and tipped them into the compost bin under the sink. Her menfolk were beautiful, she said to herself with determined possessiveness. They were fine, handsome, clever, sometimes good. How she loved them, how touching she found their struggles and their enthusiasms, and even their crossness and their foolishness. But the black shadow still hung over her pride and happiness, and when she began to untie the strings of her apron, she decided against it: she wanted to seem the all-provider, to secure Michael's attention to her on this day, when it seemed so distracted.

3

Katy stood in the hall, peeling off her huge knit and her warm cap and trying to smooth her sparking hair which clung to the comb after the friction of the cold and the wool. She twisted it up into a spiky knot on top of her head and tucked her narrow silver angora sweater into the tall and tight waistband of her short skirt. She was still wearing her skin-tight trousers underneath but had exchanged her skating boots for some red high-heeled shoes. Her peaky face with the unusual high colour in two small patches on her cheeks looked back blankly from the mirror. The silver star had fallen from her cheek. Behind her in the frame, Timmo passed, walking in his plimsolls with a slightly pigeon-toed lollop and his head poked forward. She nodded to his reflection; he raised a hand hip-level, in salute, and turned to go upstairs.

When she turned from the mirror, she saw through the open doorway of the kitchen Michael joking with Viola near the table. He was waving a piece of food in her face and grinning. Then he popped it in his mouth and, laughing, left the kitchen. Viola's expression, as she followed his figure out of the room into the hall where Katy was standing, turned Katy's heart over. She had never in her life known anyone as well as they seemed to know each other. She moved away quickly, but not quickly enough, and Michael stood beside her telling her the place for her sweater was in his study. Then he steered her into the sitting-room. She wanted to lean against him and steal the nourishment of his closeness to his wife and, at the same time, she revolted against his betrayal with her.

Viola was so much older than she had thought, and her age

made her vulnerable. Michael, in the long limbo of men's protracted youth, had not struck her as middle-aged; rather, it was his condition as a teacher that set him above her. But Viola was indisputably Katy's elder, and beside Michael she seemed his elder too. Thirty-nine years had spared his quick, mischievous smile, but her expressions played on her softly moulded features with the slowness and subtlety of many-layered experience. She looked mellow, in spite of her vivacity, and, above all, practised at being with Michael. Katy had reckoned with none of this beforehand. On the strength of Michael's need for her, she had imagined that he and his wife would behave as if they were estranged.

When Michael lifted the cotton T-shirt she wore as a vest and cupped her small breasts with his hands to kiss them, one nipple, then the other, and said, 'Your breasts are beautiful', she realised now that she had imagined his experience of her was unique; when he touched the inside skin of her arm, where it was fine-grained and blue with the tributaries of her veins, and said, 'So soft, so warm', she had thought he was bringing her close to him because he did not have closeness elsewhere. When he said, caressing her with his fingers, 'You little swamp!' she thought such words, with their power to make her molten, were made up for her. She had never thought to ask him if he slept with his wife. She had simply assumed that a marriage that had lasted eighteen years would be a cracked husk. Timmo had not surprised her at all, when broodingly on the river he suggested the barrenness of his parents' union. But in their interaction, and above all in the readiness with which Viola responded to Michael's joking, Katy realised otherwise.

'Little one,' said Michael under his breath, as she swayed towards him. 'Not good?'

Katy fought back again the pricking in her eyes. 'If you go on saying that, I'll go crazy.'

'I have to keep her calm, you know.'

'Now you're keeping me calm, too.'

'It's not the same,' He sighed. 'You are so precious to me.' He was whispering.

'I'm just your bit on the side.' She almost shouted. She was furious with herself. Why this self-pity? She looked up at him, at his expression of distress, and scorn flashed through her. He wasn't even her lover; with his half-baked desire, his lukewarm lack of nerve. She hated him for dangling, and turned brusquely to join a group of friends and instantly felt remorse at her reproachful, dishonest petulance.

Viola, in the kitchen doorway, felt suddenly very, very cold. She wanted to run after Michael and say to him, Michael, I'm frightened. Michael, what are you doing? I'm on your side, I still am. Please don't think that I've abandoned you because I've laughed at you. Please, please. Something with hooks instead of hands was clutching at her and the points were scooping the marrow out of the innermost part of her.

Jimmy came to find her. She was leaning on the kitchen table. The warmth wasn't coming back.

'Forget this hostess business,' he said. 'You're missed in there.'

'Oh, Jimmy,' said Viola. But she followed him into the sitting-room.

She picked out Michael by his laugh. He was standing in a group, raising his eyebrows and tilting his head in reaction to the talk, and every now and then letting his perpetual smile break into a huge guffaw. He looked hectic, but at the same time, Viola thought with anger, completely complacent. She hated that self-congratulatory ease of manner now, as ineptly timed as once before.

The poet had been born seventy years ago with the birth cord around his neck, and he was singing, seated cross-legged on the dais at the far end of the ceremonial hall. His recitative was low and uninflected; at his right knee stood a finger drum, on which he lightly tapped out the measure of his verse. His eyes were open, streaming. The weeping coursed down over rough red scaly troughs in his cheeks, and he made no effort to stem their flow or wipe away their trace. He chanted, and there was no corresponding choking in his tone. The voice was high, steady and monotonous.

Around him, on low stools, sat the elders of the village. The hull roof above was lofty, and the rafters were carved and painted vermilion and gold.

He was singing of the girl's defiance. How she resisted the charges made against her unto death. And of the family's glory, and of how their daughter's heroic fortitude would for ever be remembered. Now and then, as he sang, one of the elders nodded slowly, or touched his knee with his fan as if in assent.

Sweetmeats were being passed around during the recital – baked rice, dyed pink and pistachio, and decorated with cut flowers. Viola had little appetite for them. Their sweetness stabbed at her teeth.

Her eyes kept straying from the chanter to the antechamber. The bird-boned body was lying there, on a bed of frangipani petals to counteract the death reek.

'I can't understand their attitude,' Viola had protested. 'How can they be *glad*?'

'They believe her soul lives on,' said Michael, heavily. 'She'll come back in a higher state of consciousness, on account of the purity of her life this time round.'

'Yes, yes,' said Viola. 'But not to grieve at all?'

'Grief, bereavement, love. They experience them differently. They are different. Why can't you accept that? What could I have done? What? You tell me.'

'I don't know,' Viola answered, limply. 'You could have told someone. It can't be legal.'

'Bah!' said Michael, 'Rot. Do you think that if a law differs from established custom it can have any force?'

A child was skipping through the seated audience. Michael sat upright, his eyes suddenly bright. The child threaded her way over the thin painted mats of coconut fibre and came up to him. She held up a garland of flowers, frangipani again. Michael bent his head to receive it. On the dais, the elders smiled and nodded. 'Tell your grandfathers I am honoured,' Michael muttered, in Idia. 'Most honoured to be mentioned in the chronicles of your dynasty.'

Viola, seeing a muscle work in the corner of Michael's mouth, touched his hand.

Michael's eyes did not turn to her. He held the unfocussed gaze of the singer on the platform, and tears started in his eyes too as, unblinking, he listened, almost quivering with the intensity of his concentration, to the words of the singer.

He would not let Viola slip her hand in his, so she squeezed awkwardly, her hand laid over his. She was softened by his offering of tears, a propitiation for the part they had played. Or rather, as she saw it, for the part they had not played, their culpable non-participation. Blood is shed, she thought, and we are the pilgrims in the temple of art who never smell its smell.

Michael nudged her. 'That was the part about me,' he whispered.

Viola raised her eyebrows.

'Yes, about the stranger who came and saw the girl's bravery and loyalty . . .' he bent closer so his mouth was in Viola's hair, 'and will leave and tell others of her and of the glory of her line. To the four quarters of the earth, how she was falsely accused, and did not yield. Yes, *Relaganou*, the Stranger. Hence the wreath.'

He fingered it, and a small smile played on his lips. There was a certain wryness in his smile, but there was gratification too.

The fair-haired girl was saying that the pill was made out of the hormones of pregnant cows. 'It's so dangerous,' she went on. 'Women are only employed in pill factories after they've passed the menopause.'

Someone protested her indignation was groundless.

'Rotten pig,' the girl rejoined. She described the picture she had seen in the newspaper: 'A huge vat, boiling and bubbling, and several old women wearing protective gear stirring it with long poles.'

'You're just squeamish,' said someone else. 'But I admit I'm not the one who has to swallow that pill – hah!' He laughed, pleasantly. 'Thank God.'

Another girl joined in. She was trying to be a vegetarian. 'Ugh! People who shoot make me sick!' The first girl echoed her.

'You're just ostriches,' the first boy said. 'Man is a hunter. You can't enjoy *filet mignon* and get all coy about shooting.' He bared his teeth and snapped a few times.

The girls laughed.

Viola seated herself on the arm of the sofa, very near Katy's head. Katy was still eating, poking rather absent-mindedly at the food on her plate. She had remained silent throughout the conversation.

Viola leant over her and said, 'The issue really facing you young people is sex. There's no doubt about that. Much more than whether to eat meat or not.'

Katy's eyes were down; she pressed her lips together.

'The pill has made the lives of young women like you', Viola went on, 'impossibly complicated. So many decisions. We didn't have so much freedom to choose. I got pregnant with Timmo without really giving it a thought, and then we got married. It was as simple as that.' The lie was intended to depict her strength to Kathy.

'I don't know what I'd do without the pill,' said the fair-haired girl.

The second girl seconded her. 'It's a freedom I can't do without.' She grinned.

White-faced, Katy looked up. Viola returned her look, coaxingly. After a pause, Katy said, quietly, 'I don't believe in the pill, actually. I don't take it.' Then, very low, she added, 'That's not the reason we're different, people your age and us.'

Viola shrank into herself. She was scared.

Katy regretted her tetchiness. Aloud, to the company, she said, 'I think the pill is probably very bad for people. I think that in fifty years' time people will consider it some hysteria we all suffered from, like witch-hunting madness in the seventeenth century. With women the victims again.'

'Why do you think that?' Viola spoke again, confidentially to Katy.

Katy lowered her voice in answer, 'The pill doesn't really clarify choice. Or at least it's not used that way. It makes choosing unnecessary.' She knew this after all: Tony, Michael, the single afternoon, yes, she'd given it up because of her drifting then, without volition.

Viola's gaze sharpened. 'How exactly?'

'Because it's easy to drift, not to choose, to be lazy. To say, well, nothing can happen, so I'll take what comes.'

'I thought the pill was the ultimate weapon of liberation?'

'It hasn't turned out like that, has it? Do you notice any real, deep change?'

Viola thought, women used to have babies when they didn't want them, now they can't have them when they do. But she did not speak aloud. Out of fear she said, 'But you can't want to have children, at your age?'

'No, no,' said Katy. 'The only real liberation I think . . .' she coughed at her own intensity, viewed in the hearing of so many, 'is to pick and choose. To discriminate, to take risks. Not to float around, letting things happen that can have no consequences because of that.'

She was slightly pink with her sudden self-laceration, and on the sofa the conversation was resumed, excluding her. Viola, seizing her moment, sent someone off to fetch some wine, and with sudden staccato courage looked into her empty glass and said, under her breath, 'Michael isn't an easy or a gentle man, you know.'

Katy averted her face sharply; her thin shoulders hugged her cheeks. At all costs, she must not cry. 'But the real problem', Katy pursued, irrelevantly, 'isn't any of these questions, none at all. It's the bomb.'

'Ah, yes, the bomb. Michael's been schooling you well.'

Again the pale eyes, seeking deliverance, flickered to find hers and hold her for a moment; Viola felt sick. 'I'd forgotten', she said, looking into the girl's sorrow, 'how cruel and pointless life seems when you're young. The feeling fades, you know.'

'But I don't want the feeling to fade. I want to go on caring.'

Viola smiled to herself with bitterness. I like you, you funny, tense, fierce girl, she thought. Then she quailed. She isn't just a desire, but an image of all that Michael desires. 'Michael is keen on caring. Oh yes.' She paused. 'But he killed a witch. He let her die, right under his nose.'

Katy's body looked clenched, like the frozen trees in their stricken postures.

But Viola had had too much wine to stop. 'In Palau. He wouldn't intervene. He loves to care too. Yes, yes. But when this girl was dying, he wouldn't do anything to help her. They were keeping her in a hut with no food . . .' Katy gripped the cuffs of her sweater and pulled the sleeves wretchedly over her hands, gnawing at the selvage with her ragged fingertips. 'They wanted her to confess to witchcraft. But she wouldn't. Then the family put Michael in their chronicles. And he . . .' Viola's voice went thin and croaky, 'he was *pleased*.'

'Oh no,' Katy's mouth formed the syllables, but emitted no sound.

'Oh yes. It was some kind of power struggle. At least that's how Michael saw it. If she'd given in and confessed, the priests would have been proved right. But she didn't, so they failed.' Viola suddenly gave a thick, cruel laugh. 'They wanted to starve her into submission and she turned it into a hunger strike.'

Katy's eyes hunted the room beyond Viola, leaning in so close to her.

'I was there,' Viola continued, with the same queer, cruel laugh. 'I never told Michael this, but I used to take food to her. She never ate it.' She paused, and her voice softened. 'I wanted her to live. More than anything.'

'She died?' Katy was hardly audible.

Viola knew she was being monstrously unfair and was jubilant. It was taking effect. 'Yes, she wasted away. And she was beautiful. And young. Yes, she had everything before her.'

'Did ... did he write about it?'

'Who? Michael?' Viola noticed Katy found his name difficult to say.

Katy swallowed, nodding.

'Haven't you read his book? Why yes, there's a chapter about this, the way the aristocracy in Palau used the accusation of witchcraft to gain their own ends. I'm surprised ... I mean, I'm surprised you haven't read it.'

'He told me about ... about being in the chronicle. But not why. Not exactly.' She had dropped her guard, admitted she knew Michael well enough to have heard this.

Viola nodded. 'I was there, I saw it all. I'd stand there, willing her to eat, with all my strength. But it was no good.'

Michael saw Viola talking to Katy; his wife's face was flushed with wine and she was smiling, showing her teeth in the way she did when she was strained. Katy's eyes flickered in her blanched face. With assumed ease of manner, he came up to them.

'Having fun?' he asked, and noticed his crassness too late.

Viola said, as if biting down on a gag, 'Yes, thanks.'

Michael watched her turn and leave them. His hands hung helplessly and seemed to Katy to twitch, as if he wanted to stop Viola going from him.

Katy looked down at her nails. She had picked at the exposed endoderm of her fingertips until it was raw.

She began telling Michael what Viola had been saying. She felt extraordinarily tender towards Viola. It amazed her to be taken in earnest, it gave her entanglement with Michael and its baffling peripheral character a seriousness which validated her more than she had ever felt with him. Where she had expected to feel indifference, she felt empathy. To Katy Viola seemed warm and honest, with her smile lines around her generous mouth, and her transparently thin creased skin under her eyes; and those eyes that had sought out Katy's own veiled gaze were large and clear and comforting, the way they said, I know everything, and I'm not angry. I'm sad. Viola nodded her head with a kind of nervous vitality when she talked, and Katy was touched: she had not expected to be spoken to with anything but social politeness. But above all she was disorientated by the complicity Viola had instantly engendered between them by her confidences; Michael himself, after all, had told her less.

Previously she had always attended upon Michael's wishes and not her own. He had inscribed the circle of his longing around her, and she had felt bound to remain inside it, because his craving seemed too powerful to frustrate. He made her feel essential to him, and his talkative, ebullient company was usually enough for her. But at Whitelode wraiths of his life apart from her took on substance. She saw how naïvely she had assumed that his wife meant little to him if he cared so strongly about someone like herself. His gaiety burned as brightly in the company of others, and was not lit up by her presence alone. His home, with its postcard-littered cork boards and old sofa covers and shelves of favourite reading, was an edifice he had built, not on his own as he had their love affair, but with Viola. She felt herself plunging helter-skelter as in a nightmare down some slippery treacherous surface and crashing against the unbroken rampart of their shared years. It had always been with a sense of obligation that she had gone to each rendezvous, to satisfy his spoken appetite for her. But now her head spun as she saw how well rooted he was elsewhere. It was she who had a need for the kind of loving he gave her, to be coddled and cajoled, played with and amused.

Katy mumbled something to Michael about his book, in the form of a disjointed question about the witch of whom Viola had spoken. Midway she glanced at him furtively. He was not looking at her. His gaze was searching the room, and his hand was on her arm.

'Oh, that,' he said. 'I'll tell you all about that some other time.' He bent to her ear. 'I think we can slip out now. Go to the bathroom. I'm coming.'

He gave her a little push. Biting her nails, Katy began leaving the room. As she passed, she heard someone describing to Wilton how her landlady had retrieved some dried-up roses she'd put in the rubbish bin and planted them like soldiers, all in a row in the front garden, and hoped they would sprout. The student was laughing about it. 'Dead roses!'.

'It's not impossible: a dead twig will sprout,' Wilton rejoined, and the girl's laughter faded.

Katy did not want to obey Michael. She wanted to say, 'Dead roses? Really?' But she went on. When she reached the bottom of the stairs, he caught hold of her hand.

'I was longing to be alone with you,' he muttered, through his teeth. 'Come in here.'

She followed mutely. He took her into his study. The sofa was buried under the guests' winter wraps, a muddle of hats and scarves and overcoats. There was a faintly acrid smell, of wool and water, from the skaters' damp gloves laid out to thaw on the electric radiator.

'I want you to be happy,' he said.

'Oh that,' said Katy. 'I don't expect to be.' She looked at him sharply. 'But you are, aren't you? All this.' She was standing far away from him, and she gestured at the room, through the shut door.

'No,' Michael followed her gesture with contempt. 'But I've got you.'

'You haven't got me.' Katy was fierce. 'I'm an intruder and it feels ... horrible.' She shuddered and held her thin arms tight across her chest.

'Little one,' he said, and tried to loosen her arms and take her hands and hold her. She withdrew from him and fell, as she stepped backwards, on to the heaped coats and sprawled. He followed her and tried to turn her averted head and kiss her. She kept herself twisted away from him, her lips pressed together.

'Are you sulking?' he said, lightly. 'Don't.' His tone was caressing. 'Don't you care for me just a little bit?' He held up finger and thumb, slightly parted, in front of her mute and stubborn face.

'I think I loathe you,' she said, slowly and quietly.

'Ahaha,' Michael replied. 'Ambivalence, Freudian ambivalence. Of course you do. I can take that.'

'No, she said. 'Get away from me.'

'What have I done?' His tone was still jocular.

'I don't know.' She was near to tears at the conflict inside her. 'I'm sorry.'

'Don't be sorry,' he coaxed. 'Just be happy.' Anxiety now furrowed his forehead, and he took off his glasses and contemplated her scrambling angrily to her feet. 'It's unfair on you, I know. What can I give you?'

Katy shot him a look full of fury. 'Now you're pitying me. And that's worse.'

'Why are you so angry? All of a sudden?'

She was trapped in the self-wounding cycle; she could not help her hurt and its nature. So she accused him. 'I've been thinking all week I was pregnant.'

'You know that's not possible. You're inventing things to scare yourself.'

'I wasn't scared.' Katy set her jaw.

'Of course not.' Michael desperately wanted to kiss her, to hold her body next to his more than ever. That she should have suffered on his account again filled him with tenderness. Yet her rounded shoulders and the tight wrapped arms and her closed face told him he must not touch her. 'Katy, look at me. Do.'

She turned her face to his with deliberate stiffness in her neck. 'Leave me alone, please,' she said. She looked very alarmed as she said it.

'I was wrong to want you to come,' he said, as he followed her out. 'But you see, I can't bear not seeing you.'

From the kitchen, his mother called out to Timmo, 'Darling, give me a hand.' She picked up some dirty plates and tipped the mess of stubs and ham fat and aspic on to the topmost plate to stack them smoothly. Timmo imitated her, wrinkling his nose and holding the dishes at arm's length as he scraped.

'You're rather quiet, darling,' said Viola, as they put the plates down by the sink and she lowered the door of the washing-up machine and pulled out its bottom tray. 'I must get some order here,' she went on, with an edge of desperation.

'I haven't anything interesting to say,' he replied.

'Do you think any of us have?'

'Well, I don't know how to say the things I have in my head to say.' Timmo frowned, and he hit his head with his fist. 'It makes me furious.'

'I find you very articulate. Too articulate.'

A burst of laughter came from the sitting-room. Above it, Michael's voice could be heard, booming in fierce argument, followed by slurred American speech, and interwoven with Wilton's indistinct, dignified timbre.

'But you've always been on my side,' Timmo said sullenly. 'It doesn't count.'

'It doesn't count?' Viola scraped listlessly at a plate with its pile of uneaten food. 'And no one even eats properly any more.'

'You made enough for an army.'

Viola tried to laugh but, looking at the orange sink drainer, overflowing with the salads she had finely chopped and morsels of chicken and blebs of aspic, she felt a wave of nauseating misery.

'Why does your father always get so loud?' she almost hissed. She scooped up the drainer and hit it sharply upside down into the bin with compost material for the garden.

'He's not much louder than usual,' said Timmo. He was slotting the dirty plates into the machine with a look of disgust. 'He's always carrying on and you usually laugh at it, ha, ha. It annoys the hell out of me, the way you make out nothing is happening.'

'But nothing is happening,' Viola pleaded. 'It can't be. It musn't be.' With her gloved hands she clutched her waist, and rocked for a moment. The folds of her clothes drew taut across her body.

'Yeah,' Timmo's lip curled. 'Right. I sometimes wish something would. It'd be ... honest at least. How you stand it! That scrubber.'

Viola threw her head back and breathed out hard. Then she

raised one hand to Timmo, imploring. 'Honesty is your father's chief quality. He never hides anything. I'm sure he's not really up to much with that ... that girl.' She wrung her rubber-gloved hands together and screwed up her nose as they squeaked. Then her face emptied and its soft roundedness sharpened with anguish. 'Why should you bother with this? Don't.'

She tried to direct him to busy himself with the washing up, but Timmo rightly understood her pride, for they were bound in a bond, the oldest bond of the flesh, and he replied with passion, 'I hate his corny randiness, I hate the way he rolls his eyes and pretends it's all a big joke. I hate the way he's so fucking high-minded about the Big Issues. He wanks!' He saw the tears in his mother's eyes, and her inability, gloved, to brush them away, and he sprang towards her to raise her up from her cowedness, then checked the movement and shuffled his feet again.

'Don't,' said Viola falsely. 'You mustn't talk like that about your father.'

Timmo huffed. She touched him with her gloved hand. 'I love your father, remember. He loves me. I know sometimes it doesn't seem like it. Things happen. They don't concern you.'

She knew as she spoke how involving such a rejection of his feelings of loyalty to her was, and how unfair to her son she was being now.

'I know you do.' Timmo kicked savagely at the skirting on the kitchen cupboards. 'It's dopey of you.'

'Go away and enjoy yourself,' said Viola sharply. She was furious with herself for the flaming tears in her eyes. She had wanted to tell him, and by telling him her pain to deepen his allegiance.

Timmo's hands hung loosely at his side. He shuffled his feet. 'I've got nothing to say to anyone in there.'

'Nonsense. What about joining the young people, Jimmy's friend, and that girl ... you were getting on well with her, I thought, on the river. Distract her.' *Distract her*. 'Do, darling, do.'

Timmo stood. His feet stopped shuffling. His thin nose pointed out of the kitchen window, at the ghostly lawn in the falling light of the winter afternoon. Viola was silent. Her son's tension made her realise that her outburst had breached their compact. Previously it was understood that he relied on her and made light of his reliance, and that she never laid a claim upon him. But she had, and when he spoke, she knew he understood that she had called on him to help her.

'So he's really carrying on with her?' Timmo with studied nonchalance turned to face his mother. His long dark eyes gleamed under the strand of black hair that fell across his forehead; there was a hardness to the set of his mouth. 'Fuck me.'

'I think so,' Viola swallowed and peeled off her rubber gloves and hung them up over the tin-opener on the wall. 'I'm tired,' she added. 'All that skating, at my age, and I worked on all this till late and I've used a bit too much of the . . .' She gestured at a bottle; she smiled her strained smile, with her teeth bared.

'Yeah,' said Timmo, and pushed the strand off his face. Viola tried to look at him without crying. Her lip quivered.

'You look terrific,' she said. 'I'm so proud of you. You're a real grown man now. Not my baby any more.'

Timmo dropped his gaze. He kicked again at the fitted cupboards with one worn plimsoll. Then he lifted his head to say something to his mother, but she had taken him by the arm and was putting on her vivid, self-consciously attractive look and tossing her thick hair with determined gaiety at three guests coming in to make their goodbyes.

'Not going already?' she asked.

Timmo did not speak to them but only raised a curt hand in acknowledgement of their departure. His mother caught his eye.

'I'll find a way, I swear it. I'll find a way,' he said quietly.

'No darling,' she began. But there were others in the kitchen with them and, besides, she was half-hearted about restraining him.

Her son shook his head and she wondered as she watched him take the stairs two at a time, would the restless, famishing rebellion in him be appeased avenging her.

4

'You've got a great system.' Andrew was looking over Timmo's turntable and cassette player. 'How's the output?'

'Not bad,' said Timmo. He was sitting on his bed, with his knees up under his chin and his back against the wall. Andrew had wandered in on him from the party downstairs, where he had felt alien and bored. 'Choose anything you fancy.' He pointed to the heap of cassettes and records on the floor. His face looked stretched, as if someone was tightening it over his bones.

Andrew held up a flash of laminated pink and scarlet stripes across a screaming face. 'Okay by you?'

'Fine.'

A peal of synthesised arpeggios rang out in the small room, soon followed by bursts of squealing climaxes. Timmo bounced his head to the rhythm; Andrew stood on the carpet and danced, bringing up his knees to his waist as if stamping in a wine vat. Timmo watched him. His hips were gyrating sinuously between steps and his head jouncing in a happy imitation of abandon.

'Do you rate it?' Timmo called from the bed.

'Not bad'.

'I worked for it. In McDonald's, all last summer hols.' Timmo bounded off the bed, and tapped the bobbing and shut-eyed Andrew to get his attention. 'Listen. This is the Big Mic Mac Machine. It's based on the kitchen routine in McDonald's.' Timmo put one hand on his hip and began moving along an imaginary production line, flexing his knees to the rhythm and nodding his head. His arms, bent at the elbows, pumped to the beat.

As he danced, his eyes lost the mixed quality of sullenness and slyness and he began to bark out:

'Take a burger out and flip it on the grill.
Leave it to broil while you're dipping in the fries.
Go back to burger, turn it on its side.
Shake out the fries and tip them out to drain.
Shove in the bun, scatter on the salt.
Slice the bun in two, slip in the Mac.
Take the little shovel, fill it up with fries.
Then a paper bag and shovel in the fries.
Take a bigger bag, and put in the Mac,
The fries and the milk shake, the crusty apple pie,
Coffee and two lumps, a plastic stick for stirring.
That's two pence for ketchup; there's the dispenser for
    your wipes . . .'

Timmo worked his way round the room, tapping with two pointed fingers on the bookshelves, the cupboard doors, the chairs, the bedcover, while keeping the dancing movement in his bottom, his elbows bent and shoulders high and hunched, and his legs stomping high. When the band on the cassette came to an end, he flopped back on the bed again, panting. 'Sometimes I cleared eighty quid a week! Can you believe it? With tips. The customers just loved the routine.' He had his eyes closed; his lips were smiling in spite of himself.

'Tipping in McDonald's.' exclaimed Andrew. 'I never heard of it.' He was laughing.

'Don't you bother,' Timmo drawled at him, eyes half-closed. 'But I was glad of the bread.'

Katy came into the room with a shy quietness of movement that startled Timmo. He sat up. Then his eyes sized her up, with a sudden glint. She looked through the pile of music, anxious to have a purpose for her presence. She felt the force of his examination of her through her back like heat. 'I was a bit claustrophobic downstairs,' she said, looking down. Neither boy spoke.

'Can we play this now?' she said. She held up a record, a reissue of a vintage Billie Holliday. 'I like her a lot.'

'Wait,' said Andrew. 'We can't dance to that, and I want to have a go at the Big Mic Mac Machine.'

Timmo said, 'I'm not doing it again. Once is quite enough.'

'Who asked you?' retorted Andrew.

The second band on the tape was belting out a two-stroke stomp, punctuated by squeals and trills of ecstatic pain. Andrew, beckoning to Katy, began beating out the time with his fists clenched as if his arms were pistons driving the engine of his head. 'First the burger, then the fries ...' he began to give out the chant.

Katy giggled. 'No, first the burger, and you flip it on the grill. Then ...' she turned to Timmo, 'what next?'

'You were watching?' Timmo was sulky.

'Why? Do you mind? It was great. It made me feel great. Honest.' Katy smiled shyly at him, with that surprisingly toothy look that transformed her blanched face for a moment.

From the bed, Timmo began shouting out his routine ferociously. Katy's gawky limbs stamped and kicked to the words and the beat as she followed Andrew's insinuatingly smooth movements round the room. In mid-dance, Timmo jumped up and joined them, and, bumping and jostling, they stamped around in the clutter, flinging burgers, tipping mountains of fries into enormous paper bags and scattering showers of salt from giant shakers.

Katy's eyes were shining as she collapsed, flushed and breathless, on to the carpet. Timmo flopped back on the bed; Andrew joined Katy on the floor.

'That feels really good,' Katy said, holding her hands on her stomach as it rose and fell. 'I was feeling kind of suffocated downstairs.' She rolled her eyes upwards to see Timmo. 'Can we have Lady Day now please? I can't move. Do you mind?'

The cracked bell of Billie Holliday's last years quavered

throatily over the cascade of crystal keys and the wail of alto sax as, with a tragic assurance of ruin, her voice swung wide and high on the line of the melody in a fragmented keening for her lost love:

'Every road I walk along
I walk along with you
No wonder I am lonely-y-y.
The sky is blue, the night is cold,
The moon is nooo
But love is old,
And while I'm waiting here
This heart of mine is singing,
Lover come back to me.'

Andrew took Katy's hands and pulled her to her feet. He put both his arms around her and held her as he swayed, hardly moving to the miraculous expressiveness in the singer's flawed and wavering voice.

'Did she mean it like she sounds?' Timmo wondered from the bed.

'Oh yeah,' murmured Andrew to Timmo, over Katy's shoulder. 'You can really hear her meaning it.'

'She wanted to suffer.' Timmo was speaking quietly, with the suppressed anger Katy noticed in him before. 'She probably thought being able to suffer made her a better human being.'

'But it did.' Katy, now turned by Andrew, looked around his shoulder at Timmo.

'I don't think so.' He again jumped off the bed. 'Not at all. I think suffering stinks. It never made anyone better. That's all a huge hype.' In his socks, he padded over to the turntable. 'Let's have some sounds to make them jump. All those professional agonisers down below.'

The sound of a big rock band throbbed in the room; Timmo turned up the volume till the music twisted with the loudness of it. Katy clapped her hands over her ears; Andrew pushed Timmo aside. 'Don't be half-arsed,' he said. 'They're jumping enough already, with all that dancing we've been doing.'

'Yes, don't get them running up here.' Katy's voice was thin with anxiety.

'She's right,' Andrew continued. 'There's enough tension without your aggro.' He turned the sound right down, and began twisting and jumping to the beat. 'Take it easy,' he called, as he danced.

Katy joined him, gangling arms and legs weaving at angles. Timmo, at first hesitant, began high-stepping and bouncing again. As the three of them, eyes closed, shuffled around, Jimmy made himself heard. 'Having fun?' he called from the door.

Andrew's eyes opened. 'Hi,' he said. His blunt-featured face held the older man affectionately, and Jimmy's bruised look cleared.

Andrew walked up to him till he stood close by him. 'You're not sore?'

'It's a bit gloomy now that you young people have hidden yourselves away,' Jimmy said, with a slight cough. 'Come, join us. I can hardly join you.' He looked into the room genially. 'Hardly room to swing a cat, as they say.'

'We'll be down soon,' said Katy, worried. She did not want to face Michael at all.

'No,' whispered Timmo, behind her. 'Let's stay here.'

Now that she was alone with him, Katy was too self-conscious to dance any more, and she picked some books off a chair and signalled to Timmo as to where she should put them.

'Give them here,' he ordered.

'Sorry,' she said.

'It's just my Limits stuff,' he replied, more conciliatory. 'I don't want it to get mixed up.'

'What's that?' Katy caught the eagerness in Timmo's attempted look of indifference. 'Go on, give us a look.'

He jerked his head to the bed beside him, and she moved to join him. 'The beginning's small potatoes,' he said. 'It's from ages ago, when I was twelve. I just put in things like the boiling point of water, and of mercury and alcohol. Ordinary stuff, basic measurement. At sea level of course.'

On the graph paper of an exercise book were many diagrams, traced in coloured felt tips and labelled in small, spiky hand. One of the first pages was headed, 'Water'. Under it childishly drawn symbols of clouds and snow and steam were inscribed 'Condensation', 'Precipitation', with numbers and degrees noted beside them.

Timmo took the book away from Katy. 'Don't look at that one. It's boring. This one, this one is mind-blowing.' Under the heading 'Time' Katy saw a drawing of the sun, with stationer's gold stars encircling it and their distances from earth set down in a neat column of figures. Timmo tapped the page in excitement: 'These stars are the furthest we've seen from earth. And our telescopes are so powerful now that we can see beyond these stars into the void, into the dark. But we know ...' his voice grew deeper with concentration, 'we know that the darkness can't be empty. We know the universe is, well, infinite. So that means ...' he pointed to one of the gold stars with two long white fingers, as unkempt as Katy's 'that this star's light is the last to reach us, that those trillions of light years it took for its light to come to us is the limit of time itself. There is nothing earlier than that star! Nothing before it!' Timmo clutched the scrapbook and waved it, fingers whitening with excitement. 'God, that makes me feel wild! That's the Big Bang, that is!' He jabbed at one of the stars on the page.

Katy looked at the star, at the humdrum gold sticker, and was silent. Timmo twisted around to her, and dumped the book down again across their knees. His thin thigh touched hers. 'All those other stars out there, that we can't see, are more recent. They're so new their light hasn't had time to reach us. But it's on its way. Those stars'll be coming out one by one, over the centuries, or rather over the thousands of centuries. Isn't that great? Doesn't it make you reel?'

'I don't know that I get it,' Katy said hesitantly. 'But why do you do all this?' She tucked her legs under her as she continued to turn over the pages. 'It's amazing.'

Timmo's sallow face reddened slightly and he pushed both hands through the long lock of hair that fell across his forehead. 'I find everything a mess. Everyone's down and in a muddle, and when they're not, like Dad, they just seem as if they don't understand anything. It's a pain.' He got up again with a sharp, excited movement and stood face to face with her. 'But that', he pointed to the scrapbook, 'is full of things that aren't a mess. At least the things I've put in it are just so. They can't be otherwise. I love that. It's kind of . . . perfect.'

'If I started anything like this, I'd never get beyond the first pages.' Katy spoke with melancholy. 'I don't read books any more that have to be read to the end. Ends bore me. Or, rather, scare me. I like dipping. I like to read poems, especially long ones. They go on and on and it doesn't matter really about the end.' She looked up at him. 'Do you know Virgil?' Timmo shook his head, imperceptibly. 'So we're different. You're an achiever.' She sighed.

'But you're up here, you got in.'

'Yes,' she said. 'But I never finished a single question in the exams. I think I managed because so few people want to do Classics now.' But there was a glimmer of self-satisfaction in her deprecation that Timmo did not miss.

'I dunno,' he said. The diffidence concealing her pride disarmed him, it resembled so strongly his own continual assumption of uncouthness. 'I hate to do things badly. In fact, if I don't do things well, I don't do them at all. Same as Dad. He won't play me at chess any more, because I started beating him.'

'You didn't!'

'He only let it happen twice,' said Timmo, his mouth tightening to suppress his obvious pleasure. 'But twice was quite enough for Dad.'

Her pale eyes ringed with smudged kohl met Timmo's for a moment. He made, with one long pale hand, what seemed to her a gesture of refusal. He was shaking his head, and his eyes squeezed shut. She saw his father's face bent to hers when she had fallen on the ice, and Timmo's swift usurpation of his protectiveness; she saw herself leave his father's study with his father behind her, both smiling and sheepish, and the flattened sprawl of coats and scarves behind them both. Her pale-blue eyes as she had dodged Timmo's glance later were full of shame. With her legs curled up under her, sitting on his bed, her fingers twisting a corner of her thick woollen sleeve, she felt grimy, and scared.

'Why do you do it with him?' Timmo groaned.

She would have liked to say she was sorry. Instead, she mouthed, almost inaudibly, 'I feel a bit funny.' She left off fiddling with her jumper and slowly lifted her hand to him as if following the contours of his face with an appeal to reconciliation. Her lifted arms were so slender they looked as if they might snap. He moved his head to the shape her hand described, half-conscious, as if turning his face to sunlight.

'I don't know what to do,' he said quietly, before he knew what he was admitting. 'Would you do it with me?' His tense look was pulled down to cover her body and came to rest, almost awkwardly, on the fold her skirt made in the parting of her thighs.

She did not answer, but put her palm to his almost beardless cheek and he turned and seized her hand so hard she felt the anger in him and she began to kiss him to try and turn it away. She was printing apologies on him, without desire, like a guilty child. And at first he received them stiffly.

The silver light of the late afternoon lay in a slender pennant just above the seamless meeting of sky and field; it was as if a white torch was flaring behind the gauze of a painted sky drop, in its last resources just before extinction. This winter light, brittle and brief, still gleamed inside the house. Crepuscular, unearthly, it guttered and died on the narrow child bed of Timmo's room, as the girl and the youth felt each other's body begin to blaze, as their kissing left off childishness, and he remembered his mother's humbled tears and her inability, rubber-gloved and clumsy, to brush them away, and Katy committed herself to concluding those afternoons when she never had been able to fathom the tension and ambiguity of Michael's possessiveness. This way, she thought with a wrecking impulse, everything will be much simpler for me.

The word Michael used when he tried to express what Katy meant to him was 'precious': she was precious to him as the Palau palm leaf chronicles were in Palau. There was a moment, at the turn of the stairs outside his room in college, when he could distinguish her step from others' who used the staircase; till that point, all footsteps rung indeterminately on the stone. But on the turn, Katy's own pace became clear to him. Her footfalls were sharp, quick, full of the fierceness that he loved in her. When she turned the corner of the stair, he experienced a moment of reverie, lingering at his desk with his back to the door, as if he had not distinguished her from other visitors, yet alert with the anticipation of her coming, of the deprecatory twist of her sad mouth as she would greet him, of the brightness in her pale, opaque eyes. He would wait poised until her gloved hand gave its two rapid, almost urgent knocks at his heavy door, and he would then call out 'Come in' in as ordinary a tone of voice as he could command, trying to sound concentrated on his task and absent to the summons from the door.

When Katy came in, she always spoke immediately, abruptly, to forestall the threat of silence. She would comment on the magnolia's early waxen blossoms outside, or the smell of stew from the kitchens, until he went over to her. Then, like a migratory bird that flutters, eyes darting, as it is being ringed but quietens when it feels its captor's gentle handling, her tense, angular body became pliant to him. He would put his arms around her fragility and hold her head against him, where it lay, below his shoulders against his heart. He knew she could feel it beat faster, in spite of his solid, avuncular performance, and he was glad of it. His kisses sometimes brought a smile to the mouth that was so often pinched and angry, and he loved to conjure that softness in her. She was so precious to him, and he did not want to endanger her or, by giving himself over to her completely, to endanger himself. Incomplete, their union betrayed his love for his wife far less and left his ringed plover free to travel further. With an effort of will that came easily to his nature, he held himself at this distance from Katy, and though in moments of lucidity he realised his arguments were casuistry, the casuistry was a kind of grid that kept events and emotion in order.

Michael had never touched the old chronicles of Palau; he had read them in transcription only. The more ancient and precious fragments were friable and, after much negotiation, had been moved to the national museum in the capital, where a quivering needle traced its nervous line on a drum and made it possible for the curators to monitor the humidity and temperature inside the sealed glass cases. No one would ever handle the palm leaf sheets again. Tea-brown and patterned with a script like small regular seals, the chronicles had surrendered their contents to scholars but were themselves inviolate again. There had been something awesome and deeply thrilling to look at them through the glass, at these splinters of the earth's natural produce, altered twice over by human skill and now put beyond human reach deliberately. Michael could puzzle out, as he wiped his breath away from the pane where it misted, the sentences on the pages exhibited. Their laconic accountancy of deaths and battles, of children begotten and generations extended, of feast days and spirit days, of birth rites and funerals, stimulated him to tears: these withered bits of palm were true relics, numinous progenitors. Their only antecedent was reality itself.

With Katy, too, he was going back to some source beyond which there was no other. She was an original, a master manuscript, the first simulacrum of an experience he wanted to have for himself. 'The same things hurt then as now,' she had said on their first encounter. He wanted to reach into her pain. She was for him a new chronicle that was scarcely begun, but which in its bleakness and its matter-of-factness, like the Palau lists of the dead, was born from pain. It was a pain that Michael wanted to soothe by taking it to himself, because when he was Katy's age, he had been able to feel it and, since then, it had diminished. It was her fierce, unpurposeful anger against things that were not personal experiences, but were happening to other people whom she did not know or knew barely, that he wanted to reach again, that pity youth feels almost indiscriminately for the world and its evil. She was for him the world victim who remained on the face of the pathless and devastated earth, the radiated child of the bomb who, innocent of vice herself, has had humanity's primal Faustian fault visited on her in burns and blisters, contamination and disease.

Sometimes, coming into his room, her cheeks whitened in her odd spectral way and her clothes that in their provocativeness looked sometimes pretend-clothes from a fancy-dress cupboard, her hands chilly between his, that were always warm from the comfortable room in which he worked, she caught her breath before making her quick, preventive comment, and he loved her as the sum of the distressed and aimless lives that his son and his students' generation seemed condemned to lead. So he listened to her without anger or irritation, in a way he could not find in himself when it concerned Timmo because his son had refused him for so long. She had no irony, no obliqueness, no knowingness; she 'hated' and she 'loved'; when she laughed, it was because she found something funny, and not because she was covering up shame or pride. She scarcely bothered to know him, he realized, as Viola for instance knew him.

In Viola, ironical detachment had been present so soon after the beginning. He had wanted to overcome it in her and draw her to his side, but the contest between them had never been resolved, and its tension continued to tighten the bond between them. She watched him, and he fought for her alliance and participation. But even when she gave it, there was a quality of strenuousness that betrayed she was pretending. In the early days, he had been irritated when she had egged him on to further efforts in the anti-nuclear campaign. 'It's midnight. Let's go to bed. That's enough,' he'd say, over Viola's untidy head as, cross-legged on the floor, she doggedly folded CND circulars into brown envelopes, addressed them, stamped them, stacked them. 'There's just another dozen or so,' she'd reply, not looking up, every line of her body proclaiming her dedication to her task, which was, of course, his task, and her tirelessness a way of declaring her loyalty to him. Viola, engagée, was a bore.

Of course he wanted her admiration and support, but Viola never trusted his judgment with complete simplicity. And he could always feel that. Ever since that business in Palau, she had doubted the justice of his responses. Of course, he was relieved to be free from that challenging earnestness on his behalf, but her scepticism was nevertheless a continual reproach.

Katy did not examine him, and though her pain today struck him as hostile, it had always been the authenticity of her pain that touched him, and he understood that he should not have taken her to his home. Its life crushed her spirits, so no wonder she squirmed away from him when he buried her in the coats in his study. Now she was missing, and he needed to be with her, so he could make her yield again to the energy of his charm and promise him that all their intimacy would be regained when they were once again alone together.

'What the hell do you think you're doing?'

Michael fumbled up and down the jamb of the door until, finally, he found the switch. In the bed, Katy pulled the duvet over her head; her form, under the puffed covering, disappeared. Timmo jumped out and from the mess of discarded clothes round the bed pulled out his shirt, furiously pushed his arms into the sleeves and held the shirt front down with one hand above his thin legs. Quivering, he faced his father.

'Get out of here!' he shouted. 'Get out.' He came towards him. His eyes wide and black. 'Get out.'

'How dare you speak to me like that?' Michael struck out at his son, and hit him across the face. Then he took him by the shoulders and began shaking him. Timmo reached up to his father's face, to the blazing eyes and the foul, cursing mouth, and the rough edges of his nails snagged on Michael's lids as he tore the glasses away and stopped him seeing. Stopped him seeing. Behind them, Katy screamed. Holding the duvet, she struggled out of the bed and, clutching at Michael's arm, she began begging, sobbing, 'Don't hit him, please don't hit him.'

He turned on her, unfocussed. 'You little whore,' he began. Pain ripped through him like tracer fire. Her hair, straggling wet across her face from her tears, had smeared her mascara in black stains down her white cheeks, marking the tears' passage in brush strokes. He was aware there was blood on his son. He did not know how badly he had hit him, if he had underestimated his own strength, and he let Timmo go; the boy fell on the bed, clutching his arms around his chest and rocking. Katy, with an animal moan of pain, ran from the room.

Viola downstairs heard the blows and the screams and she let out a high yell that brought Jimmy running. He bolted upstairs, and Viola, her fists clenched so hard the nails bit into her palms, fell forward on the kitchen table. Her throat felt fit to burst, but her eyes burned, dry and sore. In her mouth there was a taste, salt, flesh, slightly gelatinous. She swallowed hard; it did not disappear. She had a memory of green fruit, falling. She laughed, horribly laughterless, knowing that Timmo had passed so far beyond her now, and, thinking to quieten the terrible rush of pained and hollow hilarity that was rising inside her, she poured herself a drink. The taste of amniotic new life in her mouth dissolved as she gulped down the warm sweetish wine and, with its fading, the dry burn of the loss she was bringing about resolved itself in the quietness of fast-flowing tears.

Jimmy caught hold of Michael. 'Steady, steady,' he said. And then his name, with infinite sadness, twice. The man's big body slackened as Jimmy gently took his weight.

'My glasses,' he said. His eyes, so rarely seen without the softening screen of the lenses, looked dark and frantic with blindness. Andrew, who had followed Jimmy softly, picked them up, and Jimmy opened them to help Michael fasten them to his face again. 'Oh God,' he moaned, and closed his eyes.

Jimmy led him to the chair, and gestured to Timmo to empty it of its load of books.

'What happened, come, you two?' Jimmy began brightly, then saw his tone missed the fury that still possessed his friend.

Andrew came back with water and a twist of wet towel. He gave Timmo the towel. As he did so, he bent his head near the boy and breathed from the corner of his mouth, 'Are you okay?'

Shakily, Timmo swabbed his face with the towel, then dropped it on the pillow. He fumbled for his jeans, and began trying to pull them on. Andrew made a move towards him to help him, but, barely perceptibly, Timmo shook his head. Andrew retrieved the towel and handed it to Michael. He refused it, and stood up, and though he did not know at that moment whether he were going to hurl himself on his snivelling, trembling son again or stride from the room, he felt filled with violent decisiveness as if by an elixir. Timmo, in a barely audible cry, murmured, 'Dad, Dad,' and continued rocking on his hands on the bed.

'Don't call me Dad,' Michael shot at him. The anger in him went molten at the wretched, callow weakling on the bed. 'From this day on, you're no longer my son. You're nothing to me, nothing. Do you hear?'

His eyes were hurting him. The boy was disgusting, low, mean, treacherous, shiftless, a puny fool.

'Michael, for heaven's sake.' Jimmy began pulling him out of the room. 'Take a hold of yourself.' He nodded to Andrew to help him. Together they half dragged Michael out.

Michael rubbed his burning eyes behind his glasses; he was amazed to find tears in them, and this sudden comprehension of his sorrow made him twist on Jimmy and hiss into his face, 'He's my son, my son, and she . . .'

Jimmy patted him on the shoulder. 'Michael, they're young, it doesn't mean the same any more. They're like children, they take love from wherever . . . it's the new way.' He looked across at Andrew, on Michael's other side, and grinned ruefully. 'You can't expect any differently.'

Michael moaned again. He spat out with sudden access of new vehemence, 'What love! What on earth do you think they know of love? I wish I'd killed him.'

On the half-landing, from behind the bathroom door, there came the sound of weeping. Katy's smothered tears made Michael quiver, and Jimmy, feeling the man's heavy body tremble, called out to Viola in sudden despair.

At his wife's name, Michael shook off his friend's restraining arm in anger. Andrew released him too and, alone, Michael faced Viola, pale and tear-stained at the kitchen door.

'My darling,' she whispered. At her softness, the bights of rage and pain that bound his body gave and Michael almost fell against her. She took his weight, and smiled up at him with an assurance of her continuing capability and her ever-flowing generosity.

'The blasted mess, the mess,' he cried.

Jimmy steered Andrew by the shoulder and, almost on tiptoe, they left the hall.

'Now stop it,' said Viola, pushing the big man's body up and away from her. 'Stop it. It's not the end of the world.' She sounded calm, sensible and in command.

Michael blinked at her, his eyes hurt so much. 'Yes,' he said. 'Or rather, no.' He recomposed his features so that he no longer looked as if he had been dropped, like a glass. Viola sat him down at the kitchen table and rested lightly against the table opposite him, her legs against his leg. She looked squarely at him, and pulled at the thick mop of curls on his head.

'What you need is a hot drink.'

'Don't baby me,' said Michael.

'Why not?' she replied. 'After all, it's appropriate.'

His clasped hands on the table tightened as another wave of anger crashed through him. I was so careful of her, he thought. I tried to treat her so well. And now this.

5

When Michael, propped between Jimmy and Andrew, had turned the corner of the stair, Timmo ran down the corridor to the bathroom door. A terrible cold gale seemed to be blowing through his bones, and he could not control his shakes.

'Katy,' he called, softly but desperately, through the knubbled green glass of the bathroom door panels.

She fiddled with the lock and let him in. Then she quickly replaced the bolt in the door. She was shivering too, wrapped in the duvet, and her small white face, streaked with wet hair and make-up, was haggard with pain and puzzlement.

She sat on the edge of the bath and looked up at him. 'Are you all right?' she asked, uncertainly.

'I feel a bit sick,' said Timmo.

'So do I.'

'I feel as if I've got a big hole here and it's curling up at the edges because I'm burning away.'

'God, he came at you so.' Katy pushed the hair off her face and sighed, heavily. 'I must look a real sight.'

Timmo's teeth began chattering. 'You're not all right,' she said. She turned around and opened the hot tap. It gushed into the bath; for a moment the plug skittered around the hole as she tried to push it in. 'I'm all nerves,' she said. 'I must get my clothes together.' She hugged her covering around her more tightly and looked pleadingly at him.

Timmo left, furtively, and came back with her woolly sweater and her tiny skirt. 'That's all I could see,' he said, apologetic. Katy remembered, she'd pushed her trousers and tights and pants out of sight.

It was moist and warm in the bathroom; they were softened and eased by the steam. She pulled the sweater over her head, and fastened the skirt at her waist. Half-dressed, she noticed that Timmo's knees were jigging.

'I'm fine,' he said. 'Honest.'

'Get in, it'll unknot you. Really it will.'

She tapped his thigh, listless but coquettish. He drew away. Timmo's eyes strayed to the light. Katy, catching his glance, pulled the string and plunged them into a half-light, from the door's windows on the stairs. In the humid and misty penumbra, Timmo's eyes in his bony face seemed luminously huge, like the eyes of a saint in a gold mosaic of Byzantium.

'You are beautiful, you know,' said Katy, putting out her hand to touch the smooth place in his flesh at the waist between his ribs and his pelvis. Timmo shook his head.

'And you,' he said in a thick voice.

'But we're both so skinny,' she said. 'Our hip-bones grind together. Did you feel it?' She laughed. Timmo dropped his head, caught between laughter and tears. He lowered himself quickly into the water. She took the soap and began washing him, slippery under her hands. His young body trembled again but with a different passion when her fingers washing him touched the skin, soft as an earlobe, on his rising penis.

'I'm sorry about all this,' she murmured. 'What shall we do?' She was floating, oddly insubstantial, in the back row of a seedy cinema and her story on screen was as distant and flickering in its improbable conjunctions as Timmo's far-flung stars.

He put up his arms to hold her and lifted his mouth to hers, lips pursed like a child's. She ruffled his hair, and said, 'Not here. Not now.' She took a towel from the rail and nodded to him to get out. 'Not yet.' And her sad face changed and she laughed at him, with a frank surmise of happiness for an instant.

Viola took a kitchen towel and moistened it. She wiped Michael's face carefully, and then her own. He yielded to her kindness gratefully. She told him not to worry, then said she would check the remnant of the party in the sitting-room. She looked in at the room quickly. Wilton seemed to be dozing by the fire. Jimmy came over.

'Very embarrassing, I'm sorry,' she said.

'Don't go letting him down, Viola,' he replied, sharply.

'I'm not,' she flashed back. 'I'm letting him think I don't know.' She laughed. 'That it's just he minds Timmo's bad behaviour. But we know better. Yes we do.'

Jimmy was serious and spoke to her quietly. 'He needs your support. No irony, Viola, not this time, not at his expense. He's a man with real scruples, and that's something. Thank God for it in these lukewarm days.' He was patient but angry. 'And you're the first to benefit, you know that.'

Wilton opened his eyes, blearily, and stretched. 'A very pleasant nap, very pleasant.'

He got up slowly. As Viola left the room, she heard Jimmy and Wilton murmuring. She glanced back. Wilton had his back to the fire and was rocking on the balls of his feet. His hair was light and tangled from his sleep. He waved a courteous hand at her. 'Old wolf, young wolf. Don't give it a moment's thought, dear lady. Such an old story.'

Viola managed a small smile of gratitude and turned to cross the flagged hall. Behind her the Professor lifted his voice: 'Forgive the pedantry of an old man,' he said, 'but Homer is so beautiful, and the story of Phoinix one of the most beautiful of all.'

'Ah yes,' said Jimmy. 'Revenge.'

'I don't know about Homer,' she heard Andrew say, 'but I sure know when things get hot. And you lot are amazing! A soap opera, for real.'

Viola heard Wilton with half her mind. She dashed to the

stove and caught the boiling milk for Michael's chocolate just in time before it foamed and spilled. But Wilton's voice rang in her head and, all at once, a big wind began to blow and whirl around her, and the frescoes from the Birbarotti bathroom rushed before her eyes, and she saw the woman who implored the youth and the youth raising her up, she saw the son and his mother, the son leant on by the display of maternal distress; she heard, in the sounds of the filling hot water tank above, the sluicing water that fell shining down the back and shoulders of the young girl who had lain, arms outstretched, in the curtained bed; and in the howl and thuds she heard when she was sitting at the kitchen table, she now divined the loathsome clawed thing vomited by the older man in the fresco. Mother, son, father. Concubine. Viola's flesh stood up in bumps – the length of her arms, the small of her back, the scalp on her head – and she felt her heart race then steady into a loud beat like a calling drum. Why had she not thought of it before? Of course the *Iliad* was in the Cardinal's library, of course the frescoes told the story of the son who is cursed when at his mother's pleas he takes his father's concubine to bed.

As she sprinkled chocolate powder on to the seething milk and began to whisk it to a froth, she felt quite giddy.

'Where the hell are they?' Michael groaned from the table, and brought Viola abruptly back. 'Are they having a bath? Are there no limits?'

'Here, drink this.' Viola's voice wobbled. 'They'll be down soon. I'll go and get Timmo. In a second.'

'No,' said Michael. 'Don't go to them.' Michael rattled through his jacket and found his keys. 'I'm going myself. I'll sleep in college. Anywhere. I can't stand it another minute.'

Viola summoned her concentration. But she was bubbly with illumination and could not keep her mind on Michael's tragedy with the earnestness he needed. Obliqueness was again her vice; she could not engage with his seriousness. She wondered: why the Amazons on the north wall? No Amazon story she knew intertwined with Homer's story of sexual revenge. Had Birbarotti intended something special? The problem raced through her mind, but Michael was lurching for her attention. 'I'm leaving,' he was shouting. 'I'm leaving this minute.'

Does the son who is cursed become an outcast, the companion of other outcasts, the anomalous woman, the unmated mother?

'This minute. Do you hear? I'll sleep in college. Anywhere. I can't stand his behaviour another minute. He ... disgusts me, utterly.'

Viola pulled herself back. Elation and terror were doing battle and then, all at once, she was terribly afraid. Viola tried to keep her voice level. 'Please, don't. Don't be so unkind. What about me? Don't you ...' she faltered. To make such a direct claim on his affections was so alien to her. She made a grab for the hand with the car keys, but Michael snatched them from her and held them out of her reach, above his head.

'Stop it, stop telling me what to do and what not to do.'

Viola jumped for the keys. She was laughing and crying at the same time.

'This is absurd,' said Michael. 'I'm going.'

Viola thought she might explode with the conflict: her head felt so light and her heart weighed on her like a rock, and there she was jumping up and down in front of Michael like a goal shooter in a netball match. He turned from her, and she fell on him, tugging at his jacket and dragging her feet.

'It's really more than flesh can bear,' he said.

Viola threw her arms around him from behind as he flung open the door. The tang of evening was softer than the day. 'You haven't even got your proper coat,' she wailed. 'What's happening? I don't understand you. It'll all be all right,' she suddenly cried out. 'Please stay. Please.'

At the sound of her cries, Jimmy came running. Michael was striding across the path to his car.

'He's had so much too much to drink,' she wailed again. 'He can't go, not like that.'

Shivering just outside the porch, she hopped from foot to foot in the snow. Jimmy hailed Michael and began walking towards him. The headlights came on, the figure of Jimmy in front was sliced by the beams. Viola flung on one of the coats on the pegs beside her and ran out across the snow to the car. The headlights died as she approached. In the sudden darkness, Viola struggled to decipher the confusion in front of her. Michael fell out of the car as Jimmy got in, and began running across the lawn. His shoes kicked holes in the white pall; Jimmy came stumbling after him. They met in a kind of embrace, and Jimmy fell, scrambling. Viola raced over to them and met Michael, walking, head in arm, raging. 'Well, that the end of the keys. Jimmy threw them in the stream. And it's thawing!' He swore.

Viola couldn't prevent a gurgle of hysteria escaping her. She helped Jimmy up. 'At least one of you didn't fall in.' She looked at the black water oozing very slowly under a sludge of grey ice. 'Hopeless,' she said.

'What a farce,' said Jimmy, dusting himself down. 'If this goes on much longer, I'll collapse.' He stood and shook himself and roared with laughter. 'God, I'm frozen.'

Michael marched back into the house. 'It's really impossible,' he said, 'when a man is prevented from doing what he wants in his own house.'

Viola hurried after Michael's stiff tall form in the darkness with a kind of crazed elation pounding in her breast. She could no longer laugh or cry aloud, she was dry and sparky as if she had been transformed into a pure bolt of electricity. Fire might well flash from her fingers as it flashed from Timmo's hair when together at night they'd brush it in the dark. Her husband stalked past her into his study and shut the door. He looked broken, and the brightness in her leapt into a flame of pure pity for him.

Viola was waiting in the kitchen when Katy and Timmo came furtively downstairs. 'It's really the most extraordinary way to behave,' she said. 'You owe everyone an apology.'

Viola hated her own tone. She wanted to throw her arms around her Timmo and hold him and hug him for his intuitive and self-regardless defence of her, and thank him for it with the solidity and staunchness of her maternal love. But the preservation of her life with Michael exacted harshness, just for a while.

At first Timmo laughed at his mother's words, and with his long eyes slyly and sidelong tried to engage her humour too. But she did not relent. He grew bewildered and, fumbling, dropped his gaze. Viola said, looking at him steadily, 'You've behaved disgracefully. Hitting your father! I've never heard of such a thing.'

Timmo glanced sideways past her; he was constrained by the unseen presence of the others in the house, and her obvious performance.

'But you ... you wanted ...' he stopped, and began again, softly, 'Mum, he hit me, he started it, for God's sake.'

'That's no reason at all.'

His cheeks reddened and he backed away, almost falling against Katy who stood, in frozen embarrassment, behind him.

'You'd better go in and say you're sorry.' Viola's voice was hard and unforgiving.

Katy began stammering, 'Don't ... it's nothing to do with Timmo. It was me.'

Viola turned her gaze to her as if she had not noticed she was there before. 'And you'd better be off. Jimmy will give you a lift back to college.'

The girl looked different: her face was red, and the black-rimmed eyes stripped of paint. She seemed about fourteen years old, thought Viola, and the poignancy she felt was keen.

'I mean it, go on, do as you're told.' It was appalling, this charade of authority and hatred, this sacrifice to her need for continuity and stability in her home. But Timmo was tough with the toughness of youth; Michael far more fragile.

Timmo plucked at Katy's sleeve. 'I'm coming with you. I can't face him, not today, not tomorrow. Not ever.' He was shaking again, and his pale narrow face was anguished.

His words scared his mother; she took a step towards him and held out her hands in a gesture asking him to take them in his own. 'Tomorrow'll be different,' she was cajoling now. He mustn't leave her.

'No.' He dropped his gaze to the floor, and shuffled with his feet. 'No, Mummy.' His lips set mulishly.

Viola ran after him as he went to the door, Katy in his wake. 'Darling, don't go, not now, please.'

He looked at her. The pain in his eyes was terrible to her. 'You turned against me. You took his side. And after you said you wanted me to do something.' Reproach made him stand up to her.

Jimmy cut in, 'We're off then. Who's coming?'

Viola said, desperate, 'Timmo wants to go too now.'

Jimmy was patient, but exasperated. 'Timmo can stay with me, on the sofa in my study.'

'Thanks.' He seized a coat from the rack and pulled it on.

Katy stood shivering. 'My cloak's in there,' she whispered to Timmo, jerking her head towards the study door. 'And my sweater.'

Viola heard, and went to fetch them; Wilton's and Katy's coats were the last.

Katy bundled herself up, with the scarf wound across her mouth, but with her serious, empty eyes she searched Viola's face apprehensively. Viola's severity failed and, impulsively, she squeezed the young girl's arm. 'Dramas!' she breathed. 'It'll work out.'

'You make it all all right,' Katy breathed back through the muffler.

Viola pushed the girl away and followed the group into the boot-strewn porch. She almost manhandled Timmo as she propelled him, too, out of her door, across her threshold.

The lawn in front of the house gleamed mistily under the moon; it was in the third quarter and rising, so that it lay now like a barque just above the tufted silhouettes of the big oak in the next field. The tree's forked branches had caught it as it drifted in the current of the inky-blue night sky glinting with stars as with light on facets of water. There was a stillness over the countryside under the pure dusting of frosted snow, except for the occasional plopping, like frogs diving off lily pads in a summer pond as here and there the rising temperature loosened a part of the trees' snowshrouds into the melting stream.

From the study window Michael heard the group crunch on the cold gravel of the drive. He wanted to call out, Katy, little one, don't leave me. The sharpness of his loss burned him like acid. He opened the window quietly. The slap of white night in his face was soothing. He looked out; they did not notice him.

Viola was saying, 'It'll all be over soon, no more snow, no more whiteness.' She was whispering, to respect the stillness.

Andrew said, from the car, 'Are we splitting or not?'

Jimmy said, 'Yes, yes, come.'

Wilton, courtly and slow, thanked Viola as if he had been entertained most ordinarily. 'My respects to your husband, and my thanks. An excellent lunch.' But his small eyes pierced her, it seemed to her, with resignation.

For a moment Viola, Katy and Timmo stood together, as if winter had breathed its crystalline spirit into their blood and changed them too into white ice.

Katy shook her head wonderingly at the lawn's still expanse. 'It makes me think of doing cartwheels,' she said, slowly.

Jimmy finally lost his temper. 'Come on, you little fool,' he said, and took Katy roughly by the arm.

The doors of the car slammed.

Michael at the window as the car drew away saw Katy with her thin crooked legs and her knitted cap leap on to her hands and turn, once, twice, on the crisp and sparkling snow outside his home. Then, feeling the cold bite him too hard, he shut the window.

Viola came in. 'What do we do now?' she asked.

Michael did not answer.

'I think we should go to bed. It's only ten or just after, but it feels later.'

'It certainly does,' said Michael. He looked past her, and hung his head. 'Viola,' he began, and put his arms around her. 'Will you forgive me, I've been such an idiot.'

'For what?' said Viola. She mistook the cause of his regret on purpose. 'Timmo's fine. He can take it. It's good for him.' But she couldn't resist a moment of revenge. 'He's growing up, you know. He had to have a girl sooner or later.'

Michael was coming undone inside, he wanted to yell, 'No, no, not mine, why not another?' But he couldn't admit to Viola, not openly. Words weren't his obedient tools any more; pictures jumped unbidden in front of his eyes.

'You take things too hard, you always have. Remember? Your intensity's always scared me.' She gave a short laugh. 'So much temperament. And in a man! Wilton looked shell-shocked.'

There was something funny about Katy's face as she sprang back on to her feet when her second cartwheel was complete. There were black holes in the frost behind her, burned by contact with the warmth of her hands. She straightened her arms by her sides, with the motion of a conscientious child at a gymnastics class. But when Michael summoned up her face, under the straggling fringe across her brow, the smile of the child who has capered to please the observing adult world faded and Katy's sad mouth twisted with a loose coarseness, and her eyes, gleaming black and round, blazed with an insolence that thrilled through him.

'*Pagelanam*,' he muttered, under his breath.

'What's that?' asked Viola, taking him gently by the arm.

'Nothing,' said Michael. 'I was just remembering. Spells are binding only on the consenting.'

Born in London, Marina Warner was educated in convent schools in Egypt, Belgium, and England, went to Oxford University and read French and Italian. After travelling in Europe, the Far East, and the United States, she now lives in London, with her husband, the painter John Dewe Mathews, and her five-year-old son, Conrad Shawcross. As a writer she attempts to explore, through mythology and painting, the historical variations of thought and feeling about women's nature and identity. Her studies of the Virgin Mary cult (*Alone of All Her Sex*) and Joan of Arc (*Joan of Arc: The Image of Female Heroism*) were well received, exciting controversy and praise. She is a regular book reviewer for the *Sunday Times* in England, and broadcasts on radio and television. She has also written stories for children. *The Skating Party* is her second novel.